100
THINGS TO
KNOW ABOUT
FOOD

100
THINGS TO
KNOW ABOUT
FOOD

Written by
Sam Baer, Rachel Firth, Rose Hall,
Alice James & Jerome Martin

Illustrated by
Federico Mariani & Parko Polo

Layout and design
Jamie Ball, Freya Harrison,
Lenka Hrehova, Amy Manning, Alice Reese
Vickie Robinson & Hayley Wells

Food experts
Jenny Chandler
& Claudia Havranek

1 You can live on just one food...

but only when you're a baby.

You need to eat and drink to get **nutrients** – chemical ingredients that your body uses to build itself and stay healthy. Newborn babies can get all their nutrients – and the water they need – from **breast milk** or **formula milk**. But an adult wouldn't be able to get nearly enough.

Scientists often classify types of nutrients into separate groups. All the types of nutrients we need, even as adults, are found in breast milk and formula milk.

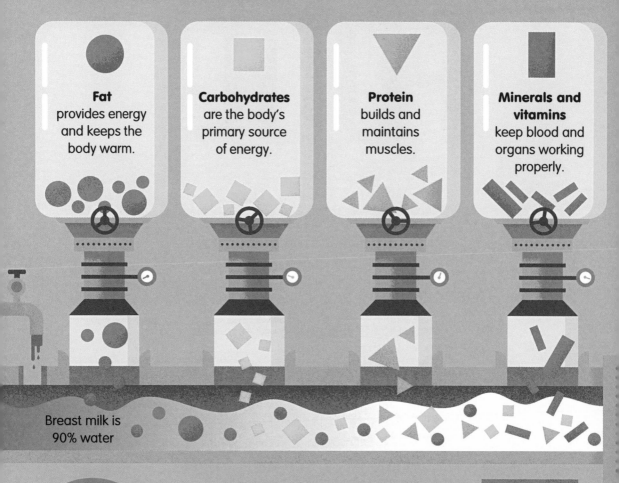

Fat
provides energy and keeps the body warm.

Carbohydrates
are the body's primary source of energy.

Protein
builds and maintains muscles.

Minerals and vitamins
keep blood and organs working properly.

Breast milk is 90% water

Also found in:
Nuts
Avocados
Some meats
Cheese

Also found in:
Rice
Bread
Pasta
Fruit

Also found in:
Meat
Fish
Tofu
Eggs

Also found in:
Fruits
Vegetables
Nuts
Seeds

Breast milk also contains things called **antibodies**, which help protect babies from infections.

You can find definitions of food words such as *nutrients* in the glossary on pages 118-121.

Milk Bar

A newborn baby can get all the nutrients it needs from a couple of bottles of milk each day.

Older babies may drink several bottles, as well as eating small amounts of food.

An adult would need to drink at least **8 full bottles** of formula a day, just to get enough energy.

Adults need far greater amounts of each nutrient than formula milk alone can provide.

2 One plant...

feeds half the planet.

For half the global population – that's 3.5 billion people – rice is the **staple food**. That is, a food that makes up the majority of a diet.

370 million acres

of the world's surface are dedicated to growing rice.

840

million tons
of rice are produced each year – that's about **35 quadrillion** (35 with 15 zeros) grains.

Rice is grown in more than

100

countries
across every continent except Antarctica.

Rice accounts for
1 in every 5
calories eaten around the world each day.

90%

of the world's rice is grown and consumed in Asia.

All types of rice come from one plant species, called *Oryza sativa*, that grows in water.

Rice is the

3rd

most produced crop in the world after corn and sugar cane.

3 The earliest known cookbook...

was baked in an oven.

About 4,000 years ago in Mesopotamia (modern-day Iraq), someone inscribed 35 recipes on tablets made of clay. The tablets were then baked to make them hard as rock – so durable that they can still be read today.

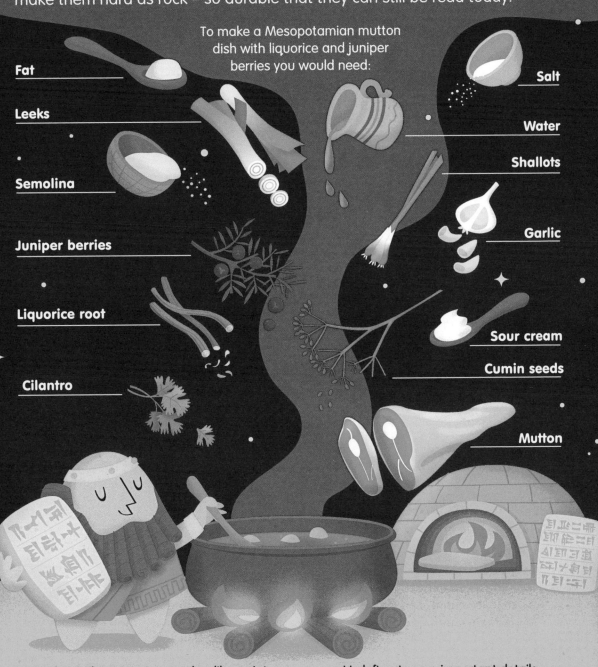

To make a Mesopotamian mutton dish with liquorice and juniper berries you would need:

Fat

Leeks

Semolina

Juniper berries

Liquorice root

Cilantro

Salt

Water

Shallots

Garlic

Sour cream

Cumin seeds

Mutton

The scribe wrote in a wedge-like script called **cuneiform**. He recorded recipes for meat broths, game pies and porridges.

He left out some important details: how much of each ingredient to use, and how to combine them.

4 80% of flavor...

is actually smell.

Human tongues can only detect a small number of **basic tastes**. But your sense of smell turns these few tastes into **millions of flavors**. Here's how it works:

1 Smelling

Food is made of chemicals. Even before you eat, you smell food as chemicals enter your nose through your nostrils. There, they bind to **smell receptors** that send messages to the **smell center** in your brain.

2 Tasting

Your tongue has around **10,000 tastebuds**, each with **100 taste receptors**. When you put food in your mouth, the receptors recognize different food chemicals, and send messages to the **taste center** in your brain.

3 Chewing

As you chew your food, more smells enter your nose through the back of your mouth.

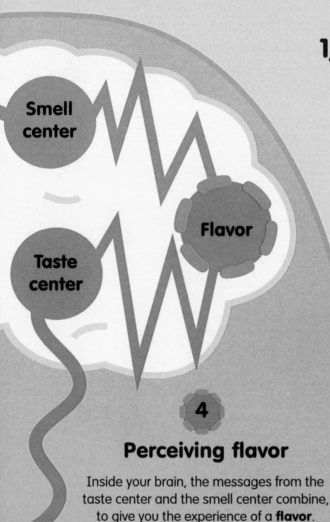

Smell center

Flavor

Taste center

4

Perceiving flavor

Inside your brain, the messages from the taste center and the smell center combine, to give you the experience of a **flavor**.

Taste ➕ Smell 🟰 Flavor

Scientists estimate the average person can distinguish

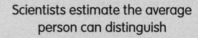
1,000,000,000,000
different smells.

Most agree that human tongues can detect

5 basic tastes:

bitter
salty
sweet
sour
savory
(also known as *umami*)

However, some scientists now think there may be more basic tastes, including starchy, metallic and menthol.

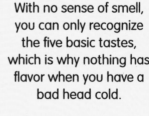

With no sense of smell, you can only recognize the five basic tastes, which is why nothing has flavor when you have a bad head cold.

5 Humans eat more sharks...

than sharks eat humans.

Movies and TV shows often portray sharks as man-eating predators. Sharks do occasionally eat humans, but they are actually killed and eaten by us much more often than we are by them.

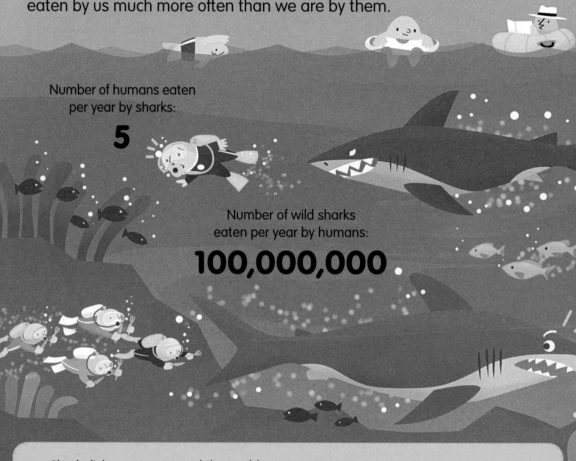

Number of humans eaten
per year by sharks:

5

Number of wild sharks
eaten per year by humans:

100,000,000

Shark dishes eaten around the world:

'Bake and shark'

in the Caribbean

'Flake and chips'

in Australia

'Shark fin soup'

in China

'Shark steak'

worldwide

There are over 1,000 different species of sharks, but several are in danger of dying out. Some countries have banned fishing these species, as well as banning cruel methods of catching sharks.

6 Camels' milk...

can be a lifesaver.

Camels' milk is more widely drunk than cows' milk in some dry parts of Africa and the Middle East. This is because camels keep making milk when they haven't drunk any water for days, so can provide food during droughts.

Cows only produce milk if they have plenty of water to drink.

Camels are so good at storing water they can still produce milk even after 20 days without a drink.

During serious droughts, crops and livestock can die.
But drinking camels' milk can keep people alive when other food is scarce.

Top countries where camels' milk is produced commercially:

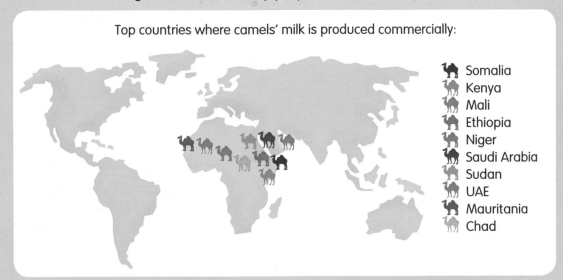

🐫 Somalia
🐫 Kenya
🐫 Mali
🐫 Ethiopia
🐫 Niger
🐫 Saudi Arabia
🐫 Sudan
🐫 UAE
🐫 Mauritania
🐫 Chad

7 Vitamins have the power...

to strengthen and protect you.

Foods contain powerful substances called **vitamins**, which each do a specific job inside your body. Together, vitamins help you grow and develop, and protect you from damage and disease.

A

Super power: Enhanced eyesight

Power source: Carrots, squash

C

Super power: Fighting disease

Power source: Citrus fruits, peppers, strawberries

Vitamin C only hangs around for a few hours, so you need to replenish supplies every day.

B₉

Code name: Folic acid

Super power: Making cells and DNA

Power source: Spinach, asparagus

Vitamin B₉ is most important for pregnant women, so their babies' brains and spines develop normally.

E

Super power: Protecting cells

Power source: Nuts, seeds

A healthy balance

Having too little of a vitamin is called a **deficiency**, and can make you very unwell.

You can also overdose on some vitamins – too much can be just as dangerous as too little.

Too little vitamin D can cause a condition called rickets, where leg bones become soft, weak and curved.

Too much vitamin D can cause kidney damage.

K

Super power: Stopping bleeding

Power source: Broccoli, sprouts

Different forms of vitamin K can be made in your intestines as well.

B₁

Code name: Thiamin

Super power: Brain power

Power source: Beans, fish

Vitamin D partners with the mineral calcium to build and strengthen bones.

B₂

Code name: Riboflavin

Super power: Energy

Power source: Chicken

D

Super power: Skeletal strength

Power source: Fish oil, eggs

8 Chocolates with gooey centers...
digest themselves.

The middle of a gooey chocolate, such as an after-dinner mint, starts as a solid. It turns into a liquid only after it has been encased in chocolate, and the middle starts digesting itself.

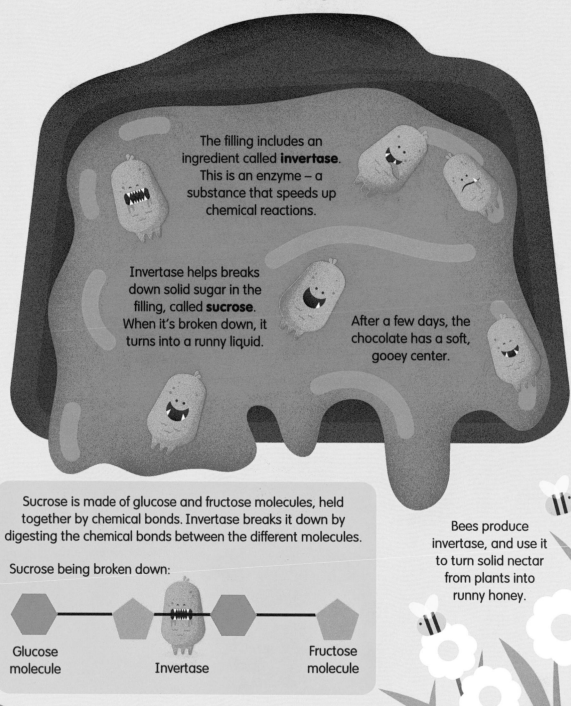

The filling includes an ingredient called **invertase**. This is an enzyme – a substance that speeds up chemical reactions.

Invertase helps breaks down solid sugar in the filling, called **sucrose**. When it's broken down, it turns into a runny liquid.

After a few days, the chocolate has a soft, gooey center.

Sucrose is made of glucose and fructose molecules, held together by chemical bonds. Invertase breaks it down by digesting the chemical bonds between the different molecules.

Bees produce invertase, and use it to turn solid nectar from plants into runny honey.

Sucrose being broken down:

Glucose molecule

Invertase

Fructose molecule

9 Cornflakes are magnetic...

because they contain pieces of ground-up iron.

Many breakfast cereals, such as cornflakes, are **fortified** – that means lots of vitamins and minerals are added to make them more nutritious. Cornflakes have iron added, which helps your blood deliver oxygen around your body.

Iron that is artificially added to foods such as cornflakes comes from microscopic, ground-up pieces of pure iron metal.

Iron is magnetic. Fortified cornflakes contain enough pure iron that a strong magnet could pick them up.

Iron particles not to scale!

For this to work, you'd need a very, very powerful magnet.

10 Your body needs food...

that it can't digest.

Plant-based foods, such as vegetables, grains and nuts, contain a substance that can't be absorbed by the human body, but which is essential to our health: **dietary fiber**.

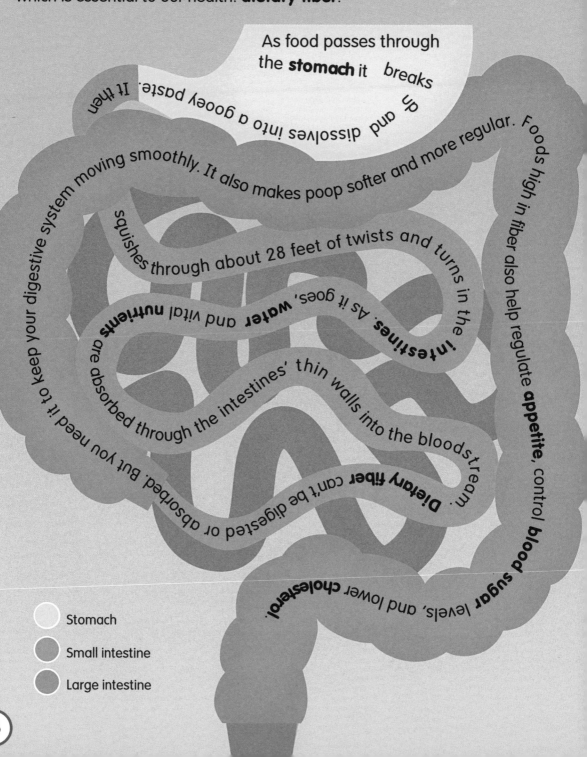

As food passes through the **stomach** it breaks up and dissolves into a gooey paste. It then squishes through about 28 feet of twists and turns in the **intestines**. As it goes, **water** and vital **nutrients** are absorbed through the intestines' thin walls into the bloodstream. **Dietary fiber** can't be digested or absorbed. But you need it to keep your digestive system moving smoothly. It also makes poop softer and more regular. Foods high in fiber also help regulate **appetite**, control **blood sugar** levels, and lower **cholesterol**.

Stomach

Small intestine

Large intestine

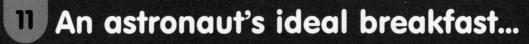

11 An astronaut's ideal breakfast...

is steak and eggs.

US astronauts preparing for early space missions only ate foods low in dietary fiber. This helped them avoid the ordeal of having to poop in a bag inside a tiny space capsule.

The very first space capsules were far too small to allow for bathroom facilities...

...so on short missions, lasting a few hours or days, astronauts just tried to hold it in.

To help, NASA developed a special diet called a **low residue diet**.

For several days before launch, astronauts ate foods low in fiber and high in protein and fat.

BREAKFAST SPECIALS

BACON, GAMMON or HAM
EGGS HOW YOU LIKE 'EM
STEAKS: T-BONE, SIRLOIN,
or RIB EYE

The protein and fat generated very little waste, and the lack of fiber made astronauts slightly constipated – ideal if you're going into orbit for a few days.

12 Sugar makes you hungrier...

if you digest it too quickly.

Everyone needs a certain amount of sugar in their diet. But some sugary foods can leave you feeling tired very quickly. Here's what happens when you eat two different types of foods.

2 The sugar goes into your blood immediately, so the level of sugar in your blood rises suddenly, giving you a burst of energy.

If you snack on jelly beans

3 Your pancreas senses the sugar in your blood, and reacts by releasing a surge of a chemical called **insulin**.

1 Sweets such as jelly beans contain **simple sugar** molecules that are digested very quickly.

2 The big molecules have to be broken down into simple sugars before they can be released into your blood.

If you snack on bread

1 Foods such as bread contain sugar too, but it's linked together into bigger molecules called **complex carbohydrates**.

White or wholegrain?

If you want to maintain a really steady release of energy, eat **wholegrain foods**, such as brown bread or brown pasta.

These contain lots of fiber – far more than white bread or pasta – which helps slow down the absorption of sugar molecules into the blood.

4 Insulin's job is to move the sugar into your cells, where sugar is made into energy. It also triggers your liver to take in and store excess sugar.

3 Breaking them down takes time, so the level of sugar in your blood rises slowly and steadily. This gives you energy for longer.

5 The big surge of insulin causes your liver to take in a lot of sugar – more than you have just eaten, in fact – so your blood sugar level falls very low.

6 This is known as a **sugar crash** and can leave you feeling hungry, tired and irritable.

13 The miracle berry...

makes lemons taste sweet.

A type of tree that grows in West Africa produces a small, red fruit known as a **miracle berry**. If you eat a miracle berry, everything you eat after it tastes sweet, even sour lemons and vinegar.

A chemical in the berry called **miraculin** binds to your tastebuds, changing the shape of receptors inside.

The receptors' changed shape makes everything you eat taste sweet for the next hour.

Scientists are working on a sweetener made from miracle berries, so that in the future, foods could contain less sugar.

14 Onions fill your eyes with acid...

which is why they make you cry.

When you cut open an onion, the cells inside it are ruptured, and a chemical reaction takes place that makes you cry.

Cutting onions releases sulfur gas, which mixes with the water in your eyes and creates mild sulfuric acid. This burns, so your eyes fill with tears to flush it out.

Cutting onions under water stops the fumes from escaping into the air, so you don't cry.

15 Chewing gum...

can help you recover from surgery.

After certain types of surgery, your digestive system can temporarily shut down, and it's not safe to eat until it recovers. Chewing something, such as gum – without swallowing – can help to kick start it again.

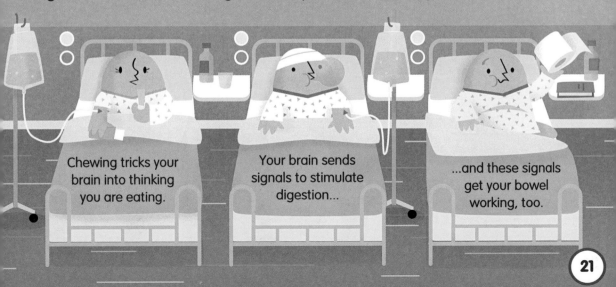

Chewing tricks your brain into thinking you are eating.

Your brain sends signals to stimulate digestion...

...and these signals get your bowel working, too.

We eat less than 1%...

of the plants that are edible.

Experts estimate there are over 350,000 plant species. Of these, around 80,000 species have some part – seeds, leaves or roots – that humans could eat. But only a fraction of these are ever eaten, and an even smaller number are mass-produced on farms.

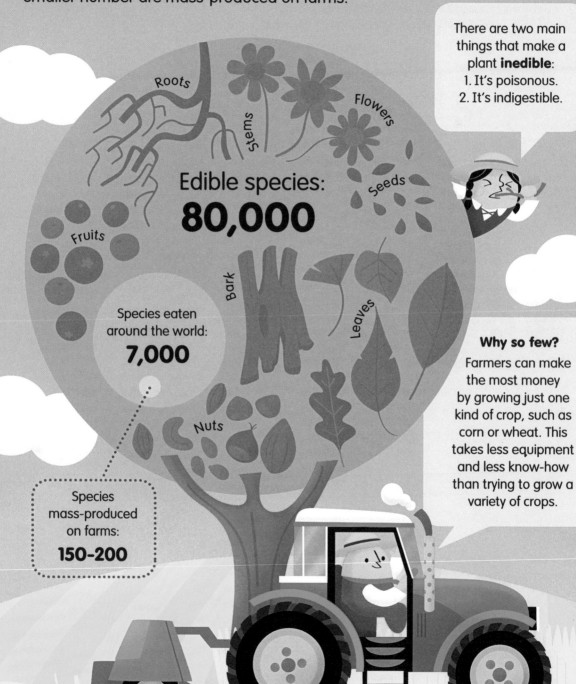

There are two main things that make a plant **inedible**:
1. It's poisonous.
2. It's indigestible.

Roots

Stems

Flowers

Seeds

Edible species:
80,000

Fruits

Bark

Leaves

Species eaten around the world:
7,000

Why so few?
Farmers can make the most money by growing just one kind of crop, such as corn or wheat. This takes less equipment and less know-how than trying to grow a variety of crops.

Nuts

Species mass-produced on farms:
150–200

17 Each pleat in a chef's hat...

represents a way to cook an egg.

Chefs' hats, known as **toques**, traditionally have 100 pleats in them.
Each pleat is said to stand for the supposed 100 ways you can cook an egg.

This is probably just a story, but different toques can have meanings.

In some kitchens they represent the standard of the chef, with the most important chefs having the most pleats...

Egg Recipes

Head chef

...or the tallest hat!

18 A single loaf of bread...

can take most of a year to make.

Bread is one of the most ancient and important foods in the world. But although many people buy a new loaf every day, it can take over nine months to turn wheat seeds in a field into bread on your table.

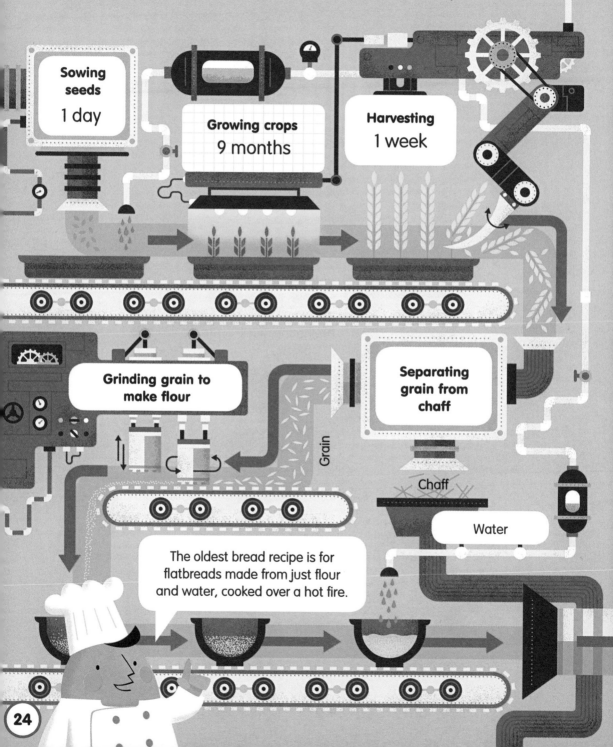

Sowing seeds

1 day

Growing crops

9 months

Harvesting

1 week

Grinding grain to make flour

Separating grain from chaff

Grain

Chaff

Water

The oldest bread recipe is for flatbreads made from just flour and water, cooked over a hot fire.

19 Yeast burps...

to make bread rise.

Adding a tiny fungus called yeast, and some sugar, to bread dough makes it rise. Yeast works by eating sugars in the mixture, and turning them into gassy bubbles of alcohol and carbon dioxide, which puff up the dough.

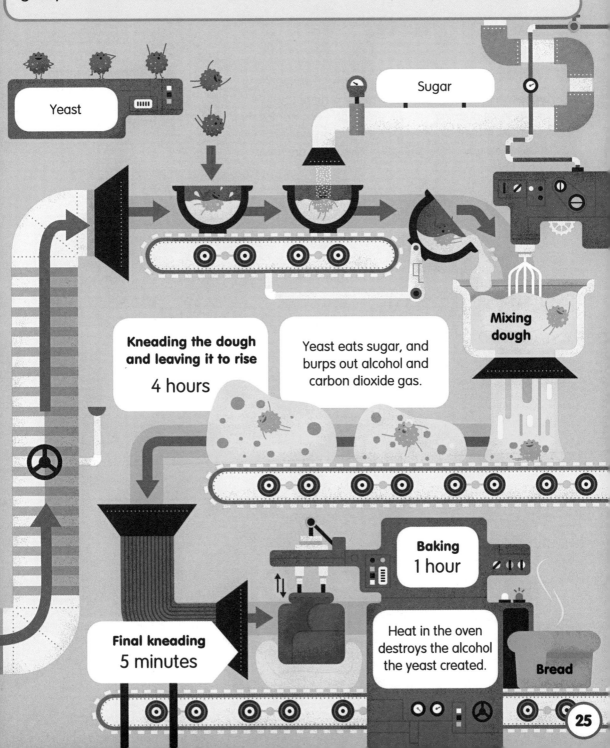

Yeast

Sugar

Mixing dough

Kneading the dough and leaving it to rise

4 hours

Yeast eats sugar, and burps out alcohol and carbon dioxide gas.

Baking

1 hour

Final kneading

5 minutes

Heat in the oven destroys the alcohol the yeast created.

Bread

20 A rainbow a day...

keeps the doctor away.

Many doctors recommend that people eat lots of colors of fruits and vegetables in their daily diet. Different colors of foods provide different chemicals and nutrients that help maintain a healthy body.

Lycopene makes many fruits and vegetables red, and helps keep your heart healthy.

Beta-carotene gives many orange and yellow fruits and vegetables their color, and is good for your skin and eyes.

Vitamin C, found in yellow and orange fruits, strengthens your body against diseases.

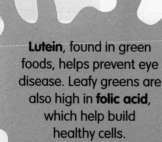

Lutein, found in green foods, helps prevent eye disease. Leafy greens are also high in **folic acid**, which help build healthy cells.

Anthocyanins make fruits and vegetables blue or purple and are believed to enhance memory and help maintain a healthy heart.

You can't be addicted to food...

but you can be addicted to eating.

When you eat, a chemical called **dopamine** is released in your brain, which makes you feel pleasure and satisfaction. It starts a subconscious cycle of feeling good, coming down and wanting to feel good – again and again.

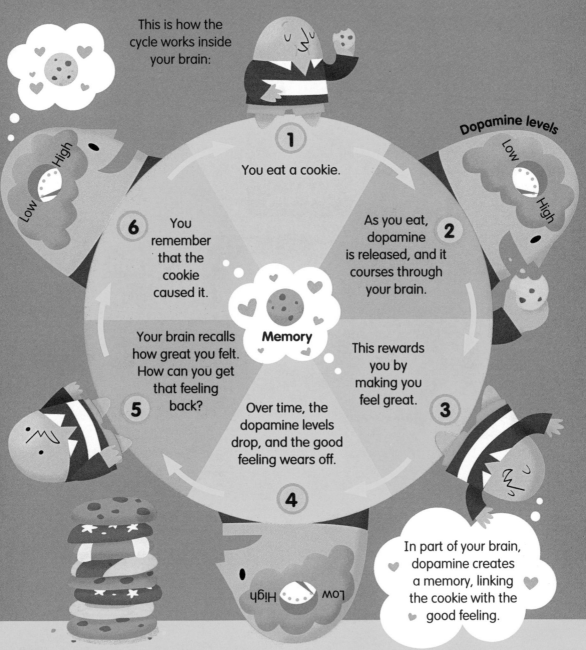

This is how the cycle works inside your brain:

Dopamine levels

1 You eat a cookie.

2 As you eat, dopamine is released, and it courses through your brain.

3 This rewards you by making you feel great.

4 Over time, the dopamine levels drop, and the good feeling wears off.

5 Your brain recalls how great you felt. How can you get that feeling back?

6 You remember that the cookie caused it.

Memory

In part of your brain, dopamine creates a memory, linking the cookie with the good feeling.

It's not the cookie itself that causes the addiction, but the process of eating and the feeling of dopamine being released. This process is known as a **reward pathway**.

and strontium in your wheat.

Just 118 chemical elements make up everything in the Universe. Lots of foods contain elements, also known as **minerals**. These pages show the 118 elements in a grid called the Periodic Table, and give examples of some foods that contain certain minerals.

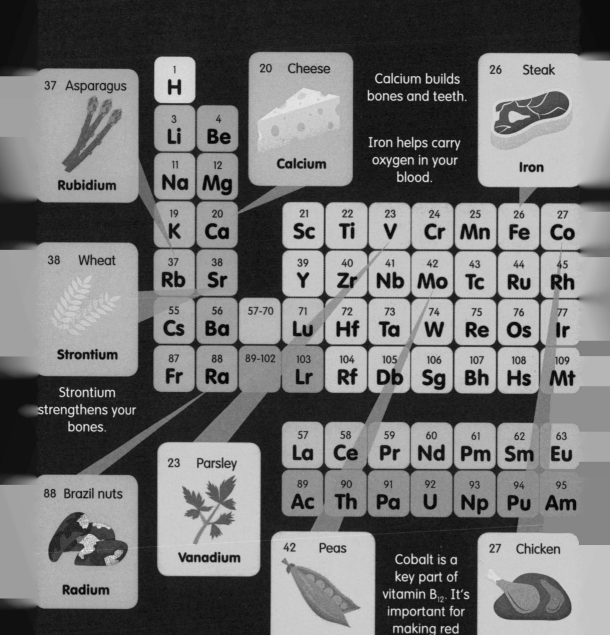

37 Asparagus

Rubidium

38 Wheat

Strontium

Strontium strengthens your bones.

88 Brazil nuts

Radium

1								
H								
3	4							
Li	**Be**							
11	12							
Na	**Mg**							

20 Cheese

Calcium

Calcium builds bones and teeth.

Iron helps carry oxygen in your blood.

26 Steak

Iron

19	20	21	22	23	24	25	26	27
K	**Ca**	**Sc**	**Ti**	**V**	**Cr**	**Mn**	**Fe**	**Co**
37	38	39	40	41	42	43	44	45
Rb	**Sr**	**Y**	**Zr**	**Nb**	**Mo**	**Tc**	**Ru**	**Rh**
55	56	57-70	71	72	73	74	75	76	77
Cs	**Ba**		**Lu**	**Hf**	**Ta**	**W**	**Re**	**Os**	**Ir**
87	88	89-102	103	104	105	106	107	108	109
Fr	**Ra**		**Lr**	**Rf**	**Db**	**Sg**	**Bh**	**Hs**	**Mt**

57	58	59	60	61	62	63
La	**Ce**	**Pr**	**Nd**	**Pm**	**Sm**	**Eu**
89	90	91	92	93	94	95
Ac	**Th**	**Pa**	**U**	**Np**	**Pu**	**Am**

23 Parsley

Vanadium

42 Peas

Molybdenum

Cobalt is a key part of vitamin B_{12}. It's important for making red blood cells.

27 Chicken

Cobalt

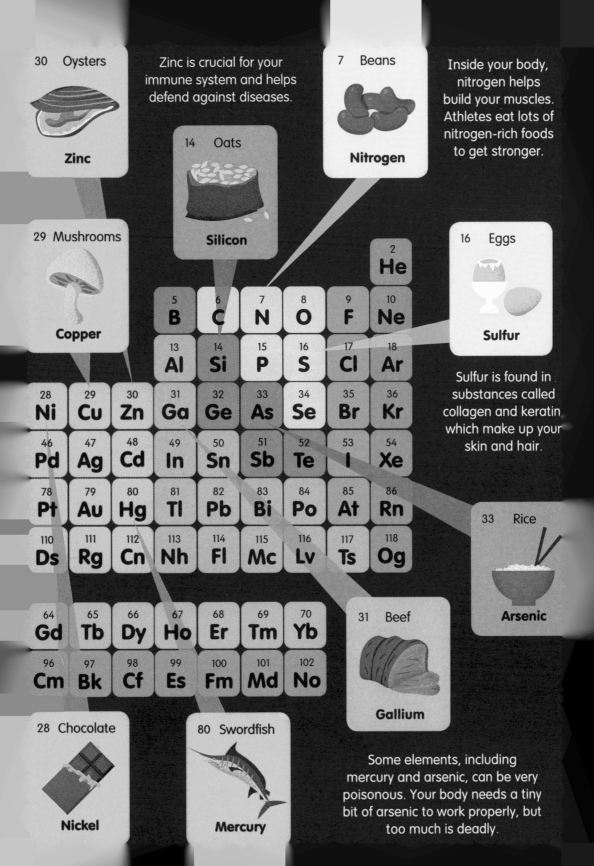

30 Oysters
Zinc

Zinc is crucial for your immune system and helps defend against diseases.

7 Beans
Nitrogen

Inside your body, nitrogen helps build your muscles. Athletes eat lots of nitrogen-rich foods to get stronger.

14 Oats
Silicon

29 Mushrooms
Copper

16 Eggs
Sulfur

Sulfur is found in substances called collagen and keratin, which make up your skin and hair.

	2 He				
5 B	6 C	7 N	8 O	9 F	10 Ne
13 Al	14 Si	15 P	16 S	17 Cl	18 Ar

28 Ni	29 Cu	30 Zn	31 Ga	32 Ge	33 As	34 Se	35 Br	36 Kr
46 Pd	47 Ag	48 Cd	49 In	50 Sn	51 Sb	52 Te	53 I	54 Xe
78 Pt	79 Au	80 Hg	81 Tl	82 Pb	83 Bi	84 Po	85 At	86 Rn
110 Ds	111 Rg	112 Cn	113 Nh	114 Fl	115 Mc	116 Lv	117 Ts	118 Og

64 Gd	65 Tb	66 Dy	67 Ho	68 Er	69 Tm	70 Yb
96 Cm	97 Bk	98 Cf	99 Es	100 Fm	101 Md	102 No

33 Rice
Arsenic

31 Beef
Gallium

28 Chocolate
Nickel

80 Swordfish
Mercury

Some elements, including mercury and arsenic, can be very poisonous. Your body needs a tiny bit of arsenic to work properly, but too much is deadly.

23 Cookies contain more energy...

than explosives.

Energy in food can be measured in **calories** and in universal units used to measure all energy called **kilojoules**. When you eat, calories are absorbed by your body and turned into the energy you need to think, move and stay alive.

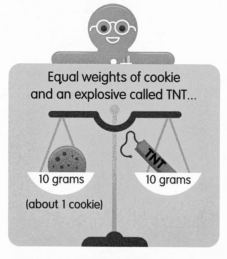

Equal weights of cookie and an explosive called TNT...

10 grams   10 grams

(about 1 cookie)

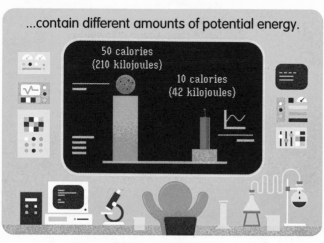

...contain different amounts of potential energy.

50 calories
(210 kilojoules)

10 calories
(42 kilojoules)

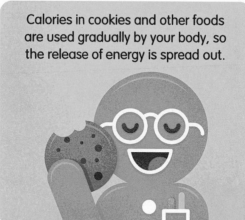

Calories in cookies and other foods are used gradually by your body, so the release of energy is spread out.

Despite having *less* energy, TNT is explosive because it releases all its energy at once.

TNT

It's the calories in food that give you the energy to RUN!

BOOM

24 Two deadly chemicals...

make the world's favorite seasoning.

Sodium and **chlorine** have crucial jobs in your body, but on their own they're too dangerous to eat. Combined, however, they make harmless **sodium chloride**: commonly known as salt.

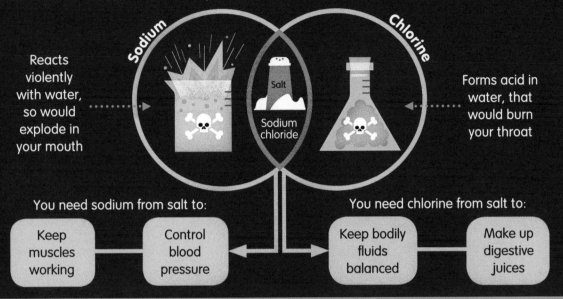

Reacts violently with water, so would explode in your mouth

Sodium

Salt

Sodium chloride

Chlorine

Forms acid in water, that would burn your throat

You need sodium from salt to:

Keep muscles working	Control blood pressure

You need chlorine from salt to:

Keep bodily fluids balanced	Make up digestive juices

25 Pineapple can help criminals...

escape detection.

Pineapples contain a corrosive substance called **bromelain**. People who handle a lot of fresh pineapple can find their fingerprints wearing away – which means they wouldn't leave incriminating prints at a crime scene.

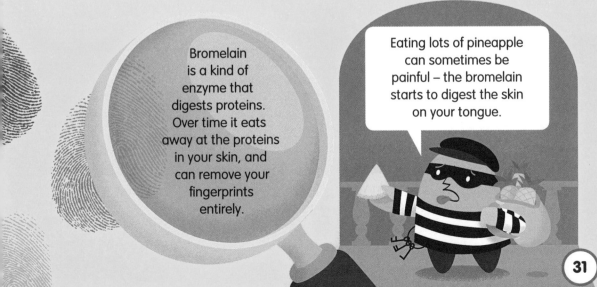

Bromelain is a kind of enzyme that digests proteins. Over time it eats away at the proteins in your skin, and can remove your fingerprints entirely.

Eating lots of pineapple can sometimes be painful – the bromelain starts to digest the skin on your tongue.

26 Carrots were purple...

until the Dutch turned them orange.

Carrots haven't always been the tasty orange vegetable we have today. The first wild carrots were bitter, white and small, and then for a long time farmers grew small purple carrots.

Follow the white arrows to see how carrots have changed over the centuries:

○ Selected carrots

● Rejected carrots

Those seeds produced a range of new carrots.

Farmers picked and ate purple carrots.

4,000 years ago, wild carrots were used in Ancient Greek medicine, rather than cooking. They were white, woody and bitter.

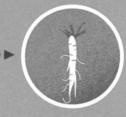

They selected seeds from the tastiest and best-shaped carrots, and grew more of them.

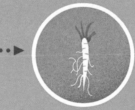

Not all carrots grew the same. Seeds from one carrot plant produced a range of shapes and sizes.

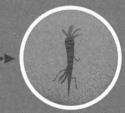

At some point, people started growing carrots to eat. They selected seeds from the tastiest, largest carrot and planted them.

Some carrots were purple. They were slightly less bitter and less woody than the white ones.

Changing what a plant or animal looks like by changing its chemical make-up is called **genetic modification (GM)**. Farmers have been doing it – on purpose and accidentally – for thousands of years.

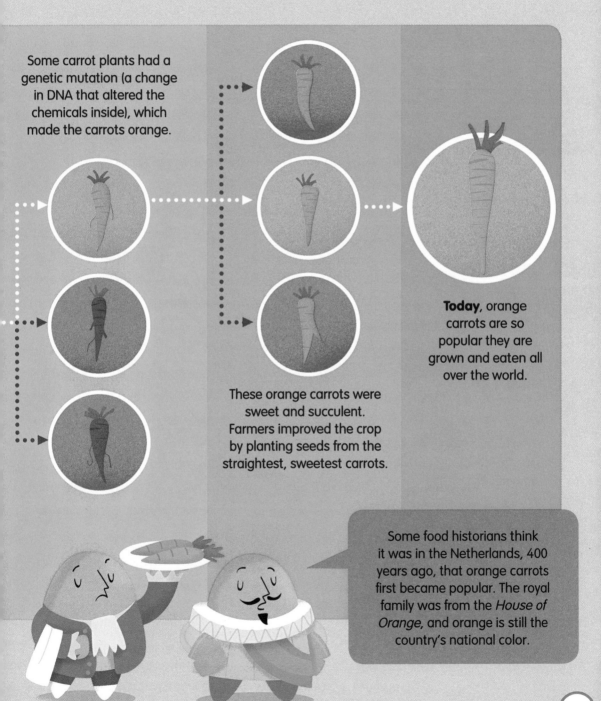

Some carrot plants had a genetic mutation (a change in DNA that altered the chemicals inside), which made the carrots orange.

These orange carrots were sweet and succulent. Farmers improved the crop by planting seeds from the straightest, sweetest carrots.

Today, orange carrots are so popular they are grown and eaten all over the world.

Some food historians think it was in the Netherlands, 400 years ago, that orange carrots first became popular. The royal family was from the *House of Orange*, and orange is still the country's national color.

27 British sailors were called limeys...

because of their diet of citrus fruit.

For centuries, a deadly disease called scurvy was the scourge of sailors on long sea journeys. People didn't know what caused it, but eating citrus fruit seemed to help protect them. Even though people knew this, it took over 150 years for scientists to work out why.

Symptoms of scurvy

- Swollen gums
- Joint pain
- Shortness of breath
- Easy bruising
- Jaundice (yellow skin)
- Swelling

Early 1500s
Explorers began to notice that eating citrus fruit seemed to help prevent scurvy.

1747
Doctor James Lind carried out the first scientific experiments showing that citrus fruit could be an effective cure.

Late 1700s
Crews were fed different diets as people tried to find the best food to prevent scurvy. One captain fed his crew fresh vegetables and barley, but mistakenly believed it was the barley that kept them healthy.

Early 1800s
The British Royal Navy started giving their sailors 'limes' (they were actually lemons) earning them the nickname 'limeys'. Scurvy was virtually wiped out.

Even in the late 1800s, many scientists still believed that scurvy was best prevented by good hygiene, regular exercise, and keeping cheerful while on long journeys.

1860
The Royal Navy believed the secret scurvy-busting ingredient was acidity. So they switched lemons for limes, which are more acidic.

1875
Men on a polar expedition drank preserved lime juice, but still got scurvy. It wasn't the acidity of the fruits that helped...

1930s
Hungarian chemist Albert Szent-Györgyi isolated **ascorbic acid (vitamin C)**. He proved that *fresh* lemons and limes contained vitamin C, and *that* was what prevented scurvy.

1930s
Scientists made the first synthetic vitamin C, which was given as a supplement to people who couldn't easily get fresh fruit.

their breast meat would be red.

Muscles that are used regularly get their energy from oxygen, which is carried to the cells by a red protein called **myoglobin**. The more myoglobin a muscle has, the redder or darker the meat from it is.

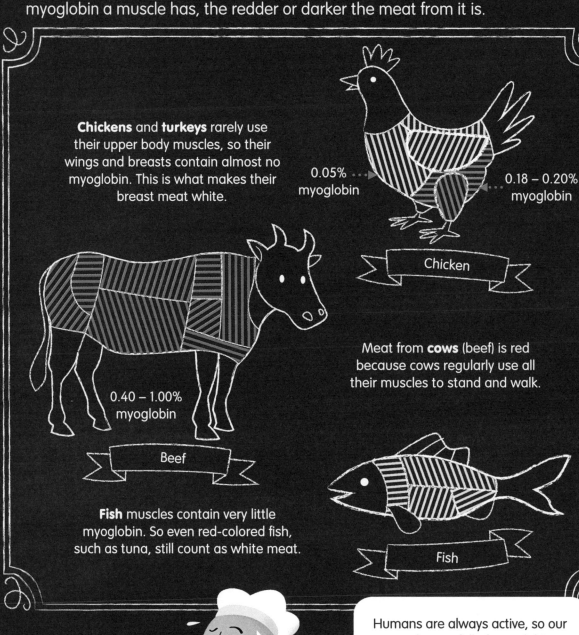

Chickens and **turkeys** rarely use their upper body muscles, so their wings and breasts contain almost no myoglobin. This is what makes their breast meat white.

0.05% myoglobin

0.18 – 0.20% myoglobin

Chicken

Meat from **cows** (beef) is red because cows regularly use all their muscles to stand and walk.

0.40 – 1.00% myoglobin

Beef

Fish muscles contain very little myoglobin. So even red-colored fish, such as tuna, still count as white meat.

Fish

Humans are always active, so our muscles are full of myoglobin.

If humans were on the menu, we would be considered red meat.

29 Lab-grown burgers...
could be coming to a supermarket near you.

In 2013, scientists in the Netherlands grew the world's first hamburger patty in a laboratory. So-called **'frankenburgers'** have never been part of a living creature, but are grown from cells taken from an animal.

1 Muscle tissue is taken from a cow, and cells are extracted from it.

2 Growth protein is added to the cells. They grow into muscle fibers.

This takes about six weeks.

3 About 20,000 muscle fibers are ground, mixed and shaped to make a burger.

Creating the first lab burger cost about 20,000 times more than a 'normal' burger costs to buy. As technology improves, the cost should decrease.

Meat grown in a lab may not sound very appealing, but it has many advantages over meat from farmed animals:

- It makes less of an impact on the environment.

- It's produced without harming animals.

- It's naturally low in fat and contains no bones.

- It contains no pesticides or growth hormones.

30 You can't untoast toast...

or unfry bacon.

During cooking, foods undergo changes that affect their chemical structure, as well as their taste, texture and appearance. Most of theses changes cannot be undone. In chemistry they are known as **irreversible reactions**.

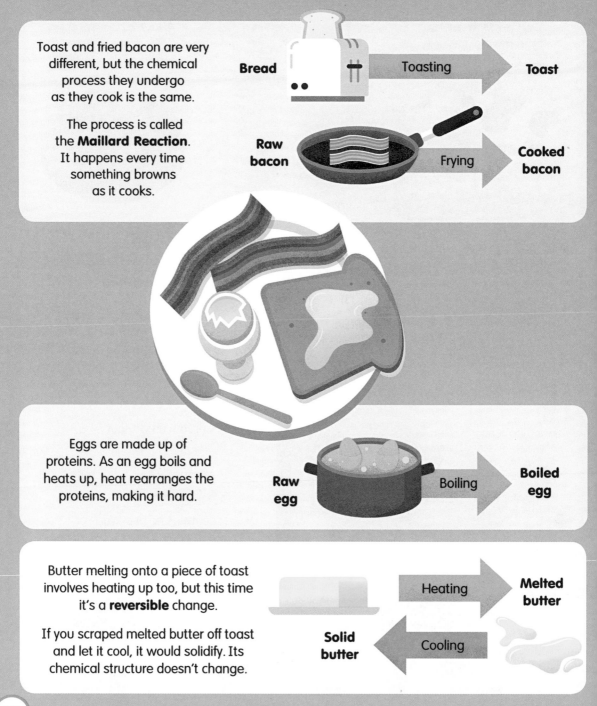

Toast and fried bacon are very different, but the chemical process they undergo as they cook is the same.

The process is called the **Maillard Reaction**. It happens every time something browns as it cooks.

Bread → Toasting → Toast

Raw bacon → Frying → Cooked bacon

Eggs are made up of proteins. As an egg boils and heats up, heat rearranges the proteins, making it hard.

Raw egg → Boiling → Boiled egg

Butter melting onto a piece of toast involves heating up too, but this time it's a **reversible** change.

If you scraped melted butter off toast and let it cool, it would solidify. Its chemical structure doesn't change.

Solid butter ← Heating → Melted butter
← Cooling

31 Beans really do...

make you gassy.

Eating beans can make you pass gas, because they contain a type of carbohydrate that is difficult to digest. Tiny bacteria living in your large intestine break it down for you, releasing gas in the process.

Beans contain complex carbohydrate molecules called **oligosaccharides**. These are strings of sugar molecules joined together.

The digestive juices in your stomach don't have the right enzymes to break down oligosaccharides, so they arrive in your intestine undigested.

Helpful bacteria living in your large intestine break down oligosaccharides into sugars, which are absorbed by your body. Gas is released as a side product.

Sometimes the gas produced contains hydrogen sulfide, which can make it smell eggy.

Passing gas is normal – an average person does it 15 times a day.

Handkerchiefs and radiators...

are both names of types of pasta.

All pasta starts as a dough made of durum wheat and water, which is then turned into one of hundreds of different shapes. Each shape is suited to a particular sauce, and has a name, which usually reflects what it looks like.

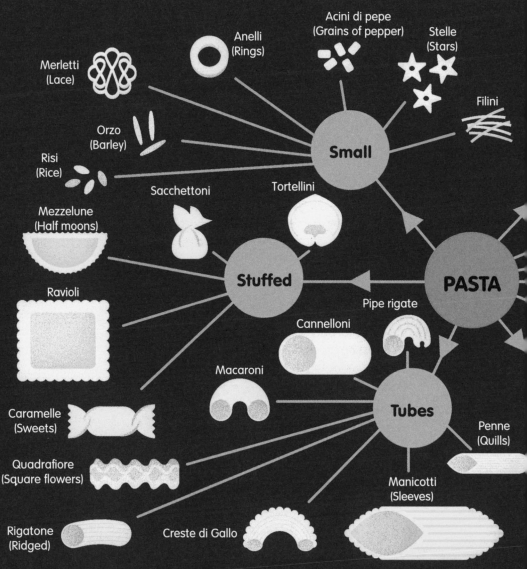

Merletti (Lace)

Anelli (Rings)

Acini di pepe (Grains of pepper)

Stelle (Stars)

Filini

Orzo (Barley)

Risi (Rice)

Small

Sacchettoni

Tortellini

Mezzelune (Half moons)

Stuffed

Ravioli

PASTA

Pipe rigate

Cannelloni

Macaroni

Caramelle (Sweets)

Tubes

Penne (Quills)

Quadrafiore (Square flowers)

Manicotti (Sleeves)

Rigatone (Ridged)

Creste di Gallo

The specific shape of the pasta determines which sauce would best accompany it.
Ridged shapes: rich tomato sauces, which stick to the ridges
Spiral shapes: pesto, which fills the twists
Shells: creamy sauces
Tubes: thick, meaty sauces, which need a sturdy pasta shape so they don't break
Long strands: oil sauces, which lubricate and separate the strands
Small: added to soups and salads

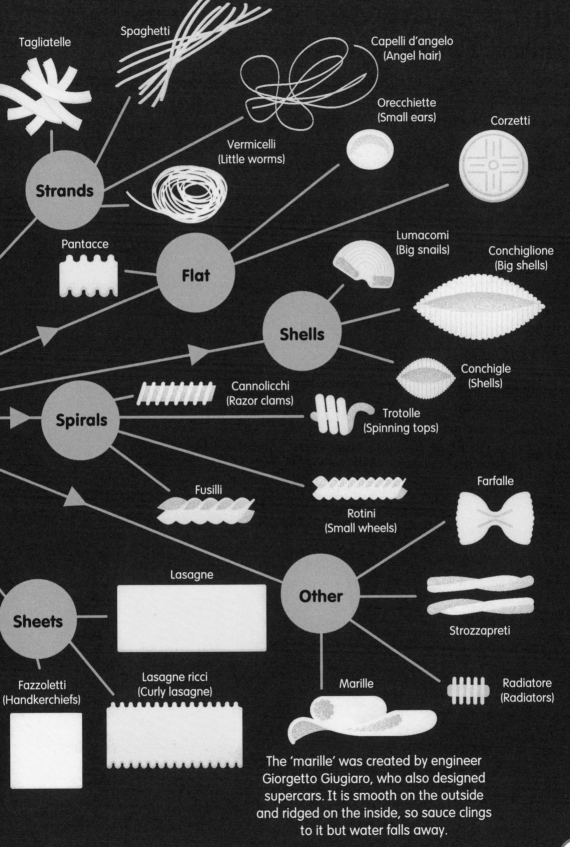

Tagliatelle

Spaghetti

Capelli d'angelo
(Angel hair)

Orecchiette
(Small ears)

Corzetti

Strands

Vermicelli
(Little worms)

Lumacomi
(Big snails)

Conchiglione
(Big shells)

Pantacce

Flat

Shells

Conchigle
(Shells)

Cannolicchi
(Razor clams)

Spirals

Trotolle
(Spinning tops)

Fusilli

Rotini
(Small wheels)

Farfalle

Lasagne

Other

Sheets

Strozzapreti

Fazzoletti
(Handkerchiefs)

Lasagne ricci
(Curly lasagne)

Marille

Radiatore
(Radiators)

The 'marille' was created by engineer
Giorgetto Giugiaro, who also designed
supercars. It is smooth on the outside
and ridged on the inside, so sauce clings
to it but water falls away.

33 The perfect apple...

is made by sticking trees together.

Apple farmers carefully engineer their trees to be the best apple-growing machines they can be. They do this in a process called **grafting**, where they stick together the best parts of different trees, to create a new, better tree.

This tree has delicious apples, but its roots are weak and it is susceptible to diseases.

This tree has solid roots and is disease-resistant, but its apples don't taste good.

Farmers take a branch from one tree...

...and wedge it into the stump of another. They fix them together using tape or glue.

The branch fuses permanently with the stump, and a new tree grows out of it.

All apple varieties originally came from one species of tree, called *Malus pumila*.

But grafting has allowed farmers to create more than 7,000 new varieties.

34 Two perfect melons...

cost more than $22,000.

In Japan, certain fruits are considered luxury gifts, so farmers spend a lot of time and effort making them perfect. But perfection has a price – and it can be pretty steep.

The highest prices are reached at auction, where it's considered lucky to buy the first fruits of the season.

T-shaped stems left attached for decoration

Densuke watermelon

- Rare black-skinned melon
- One once sold for 650,000 Japanese yen (¥) (around $5,500).

Yubari King melon

- Grown in specially designed greenhouses in Yubari
- Top-grade melons are smooth and perfectly round.
- In 2008, a pair of melons sold for ¥2.5 million (around $22,000).

Ruby Roman grapes

- Grapes the size of ping pong balls
- A bunch once sold for ¥1 million (around $8,500).

35 Square watermelons...

are designed to fit in refrigerators.

Square watermelons have been created by growing round watermelons inside glass boxes. Each melon takes on the shape of the box as it grows – ending up as a cube.

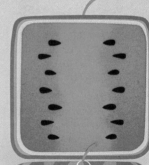

Square watermelons were first grown in Japan, where household space is often limited.

36 Red makes you hungry...
food manufacturers bet on it.

Lots of restaurants and food brands use red signs and packages to attract customers. Red is thought to make people hungry, but psychologists don't agree on the reason why. Here are three possible explanations.

Red often signifies danger, which can trigger physical reactions in our bodies. It can speed up bodily processes, including the rate we use energy, making us hungry.

We are drawn to red things because they suggest ripe fruit – a sugary energy source.

The reason isn't scientific, but cultural. We associate red with hunger *because* so much branding is red.

Look at all the red foods on this page. Do they make you feel hungry? Do they look sweet? Which theory do you agree with?

A green glass...

makes water taste cooler.

Psychologists have discovered that all sorts of things can affect how food tastes – from the color of your plates, to the kind of silverware you use.

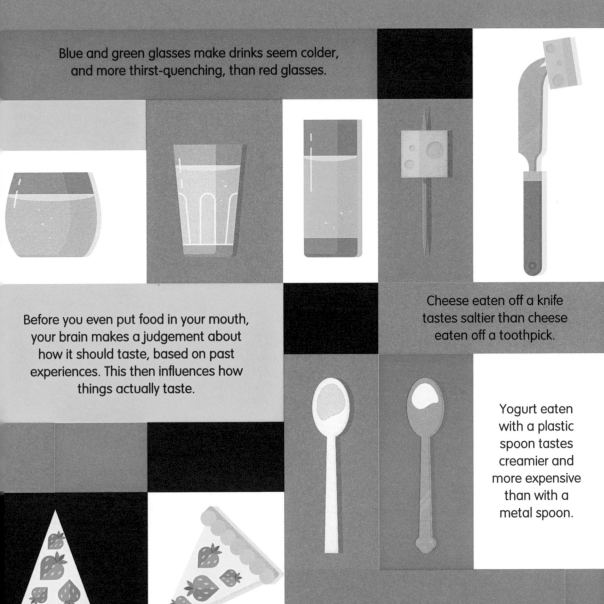

Blue and green glasses make drinks seem colder, and more thirst-quenching, than red glasses.

Before you even put food in your mouth, your brain makes a judgement about how it should taste, based on past experiences. This then influences how things actually taste.

Cheese eaten off a knife tastes saltier than cheese eaten off a toothpick.

Yogurt eaten with a plastic spoon tastes creamier and more expensive than with a metal spoon.

A strawberry dessert served on a white plate tastes much sweeter than one on a black plate.

You could test this out on your friends. Give them some yogurt on a metal spoon, then on a plastic spoon, and ask them how they compare. (But don't tell them it's the same yogurt beforehand.)

38 Teeth tell a story...

of what humans ate long ago.

Archaeologists can learn a lot about the diet and eating habits of people in the past by looking at the remains of their teeth. Features and marks on teeth tell us about what, and how, different people ate.

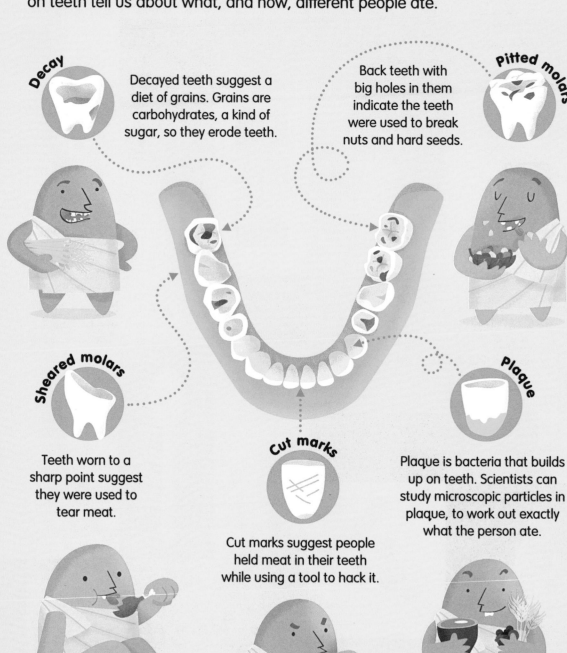

Decay

Decayed teeth suggest a diet of grains. Grains are carbohydrates, a kind of sugar, so they erode teeth.

Pitted molars

Back teeth with big holes in them indicate the teeth were used to break nuts and hard seeds.

Sheared molars

Teeth worn to a sharp point suggest they were used to tear meat.

Cut marks

Cut marks suggest people held meat in their teeth while using a tool to hack it.

Plaque

Plaque is bacteria that builds up on teeth. Scientists can study microscopic particles in plaque, to work out exactly what the person ate.

39 The top kitchen gadget of 1576...

was a dog.

Chefs in Elizabethan England specialized in roasting meat before an open fire. To make the perfect roast dinner, they relied on a special bit of kitchen equipment: a tough, short-legged, long-bodied dog bred to run in a wheel.

As the dog raced along, it turned a spit, ensuring that meat on the spit cooked evenly. Dogs worked in pairs, taking turns to run in the wheel.

These 'turnspit dogs' are mentioned in one of Shakespeare's plays, and are described in the very first book about dogs, published in 1576.

Turnspit dogs could be found in British kitchens for hundreds of years – until people invented mechanical spits, and the breed died out.

The dogs worked long hours, but they did get one day off per week. People took them to church on Sundays, to serve as foot-warmers.

40 Ketchup is both...

solid and liquid.

Anyone who's tried to get ketchup out of a glass bottle knows it can behave unpredictably – going from immovable solid to splattering liquid in the blink of an eye.

Ketchup is a blend of water, vinegar, sugar, tomato, thickeners and spices. It belongs to a category of mysterious substances called **non-Newtonian fluids**.

WATER

KETCHUP

NON-NEWTONIAN FLUIDS are unusual: sometimes they act like a liquid, and sometimes like a solid.

NEWTONIAN FLUIDS are 'normal' liquids: they pour in a smooth, regular flow.

Precisely how they act depends on how much force is being applied to them, how it's being applied, and for how long.

Other non-Newtonian fluids:

Tree resin, for example, flows like a liquid over time – but a sudden blow can make it shatter like glass.

LAVA

PAINT

BLOOD

QUICKSAND

PEANUT BUTTER

TOOTHPASTE

TREE RESIN

Ketchup has a property called **shear thinning**. This means it becomes thinner when a force such as shaking or stirring is applied.

Most of the time, moderate shaking simply won't dislodge it from the bottle. Instead, there are two more or less reliable ways to turn it from a solid into a liquid (see right).

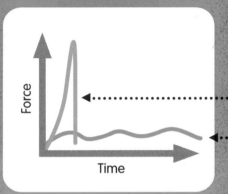

Force

Time

1

A quick, very hard blow can suddenly make ketchup 1,000 times thinner than it was before.

2

Slow, gentle shaking over a long time can gradually thin the ketchup so that it flows out.

Ketchup is so unpredicatable that even supercomputers can't tell exactly how it will flow.

41 Bug-infested biscuits...

were once a sailor's daily fare.

For hundreds of years, sailors on long journeys survived largely on rations of rock-hard and frequently bug-infested biscuits. These biscuits had one redeeming quality: they could last more than five years without spoiling.

"MERMAID'S BEST"
SHIP'S BISCUITS

Ingredients: **FLOUR** and **WATER** only

Biscuits lovingly baked again and again until hard and dry.

After several months, barrel may also contain weevils and insect larvae.

Ship's biscuits are also known as **hardtack** or **sea biscuits**, but sailors had other names for them: tooth dullers, molar breakers, sheet iron, and worm castles.

Sailors sometimes soaked the biscuits in their coffee, to make them soft enough to eat.

As an added bonus, the bugs floated to the surface and could be skimmed off.

42 Durian fruit are so smelly...

they are banned on public transportation.

Durians are big, spiky fruits that grow in Malaysia and Singapore. They are the size of melons, and smell so pungent that it's illegal in some countries to carry or eat one on buses and trains. Despite their smell, durians are enjoyed as a delicacy.

Durians are so pungent that animals can smell them from as far as half a mile (800m) away in the rainforest.

People have compared the smell of durian to:

Sewage

Old cheese

Dirty socks

Onions

Rotting meat

The smell of a banana is mainly caused by just

1

chemical, called isoamyl acetate.

The smell of a durian is caused by almost

50

different chemicals, including 4 not found anywhere else in the world.

43 A well-stocked kitchen...

can double as a first aid kit.

Some of the things we eat have scientifically proven medicinal qualities. (You should still consult a doctor before trying these remedies yourself.)

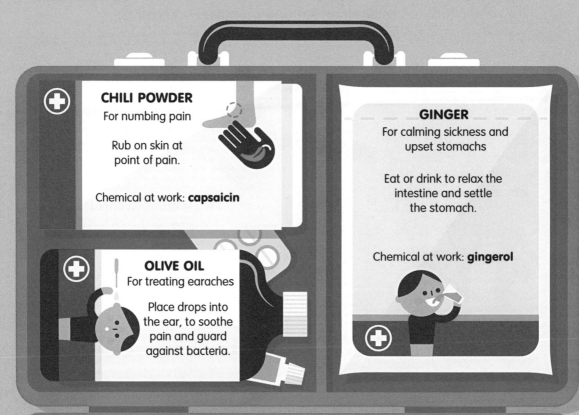

CHILI POWDER
For numbing pain

Rub on skin at point of pain.

Chemical at work: **capsaicin**

OLIVE OIL
For treating earaches

Place drops into the ear, to soothe pain and guard against bacteria.

GINGER
For calming sickness and upset stomachs

Eat or drink to relax the intestine and settle the stomach.

Chemical at work: **gingerol**

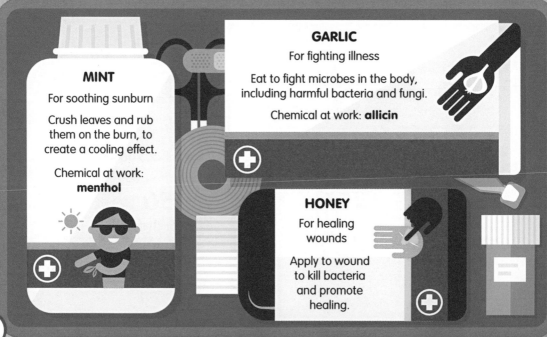

MINT
For soothing sunburn

Crush leaves and rub them on the burn, to create a cooling effect.

Chemical at work: **menthol**

GARLIC
For fighting illness

Eat to fight microbes in the body, including harmful bacteria and fungi.

Chemical at work: **allicin**

HONEY
For healing wounds

Apply to wound to kill bacteria and promote healing.

44 Antiseptic cheese...

kept farmers' wounds clean.

A type of mold is added to blue cheeses to give them a distinct, sharp flavor. The mold is called **penicillium**, and it can also be made into a medicine, called **penicillin**, used to treat infections.

Over 1,000 years ago

Blue cheese was probably created by accident, when cheese maturing underground was covered with penicillium mold from the cave or cellar floor.

French shepherds found that rubbing blue cheese into cuts and scrapes helped wounds feel better.

They didn't realize the mold was an antiseptic, stopping infections from getting inside the wound.

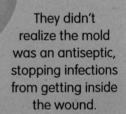

100 years ago

A Scottish biologist named **Alexander Fleming** discovered that penicillium contained a substance that killed bacteria. He called it penicillin, and since the 1940s it has been used as a medicine.

Today

Although blue cheese still contains penicillium, the cheese itself is no longer used as medicine.

Gorgonzola

Roquefort

Stilton

45 It takes a brigade...

to get a plate across the 'pass'.

Restaurants are traditionally run using the **brigade system**. Invented in the 19th century by the French chef Georges-Auguste Escoffier and inspired by military organization, it features a strict chain of command and a high degree of specialization.

The kitchen brigade was designed to streamline the cooking process in large restaurants. Even today, most fine dining kitchens use a version of the brigade.

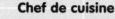

Chef de cuisine
Manages the kitchen, creates menus, purchases food, trains apprentices

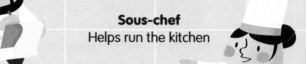

Sous-chef
Helps run the kitchen

Rôtisseur
Runs the roasting, grilling and frying station

Grillardin
Grills meats

Friturier
Fries food

The kitchen hierarchy:
(shown here on headbands)

| Chef de cuisine (head chef) |
| Sous-chef (deputy head chef) |
| Chef de partie (station manager) |
| Cuisinier (cook) |
| Commis (junior cook) |
| Apprenti (apprentice) |

Saucier
Runs the saucemaking and sautéeing station

Poissonnier
Runs the fish station

Entremetier
Runs the soups, eggs and vegetables station

Potager
Prepares soups

Legumier
Prepares vegetable dishes

Pâtissier
Runs the pastry and dessert station

Garde Manger
Runs the pantry and prepares cold dishes, salads, charcuterie

Aboyeur (Barker)
Shouts orders to the kitchen, assembles and checks dishes at the pass

Plongeur (Diver)
Washes dishes

Waiter

The pass

Table or countertop where dishes are given final touches before going to diners

Diners

46 Cream before jam...
is the correct way to prepare a scone.

Eating scones is an English tradition – but many English people disagree fiercely on how this should be done. The correct approach is to slather the scone with clotted cream, and then spoon jam on top.

Scone – a small, round, crumbly cake.

Clotted cream – a very thick, rich, gooey cream.

Jam – usually strawberry, but any berry will do.

Scone seen from above

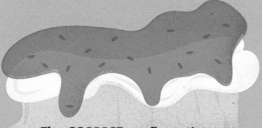

The CORRECT configuration

Traditionally, people eat scones with cream and jam during **afternoon tea**. This meal also includes dainty finger sandwiches, cakes and pastries and, of course, tea.

But the scone is a source of controversy, and England is divided along 'cream-first' and 'jam-first' lines.

In fact, English people can't even agree on how to *pronounce* scone. Does it rhyme with *own* or *on*?

is the correct way to prepare a scone.

Eating scones is an English tradition – but many English people disagree fiercely on how this should be done. The correct approach is to spread jam across the scone, and then top it off with a dollop of cream.

- ● **Scone** – a small, round, crumbly cake.

- ● **Jam** – usually strawberry, but any berry will do.

- ○ **Clotted cream** – a very thick, rich, gooey cream.

The CORRECT configuration

Scone seen from above

For some, the quarrel between 'jam-firsters' and 'cream-firsters' is linked to a geographical rivalry.

People from **Devon** spread on cream before jam. Their neighbors in **Cornwall** add jam before cream.

There are many other culinary controversies:

'Tea-firsters' versus 'Milk-firsters'

'Little-endians' versus 'Big-endians'

47 Oranges aren't orange...

when they grow in very hot places.

Orange skins only turn orange if the weather goes through cool spells as well as hot periods. So, in countries with a tropical climate, oranges stay green.

All oranges are orange on the *inside*, but start out green on the *outside*. The green color comes from a substance in the skin called **chlorophyll**.

In cooler weather, chlorophyll in orange skin is broken down. Without the green chlorophyll, the skin turns orange.

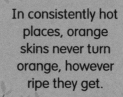

In consistently hot places, orange skins never turn orange, however ripe they get.

In hot parts of the US, if oranges stay green, farmers spray them with a gas called **ethylene** that breaks down the chlorophyll.

They do this only because orange oranges are easier to sell.

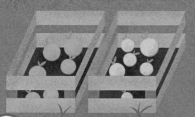

48 Kiwi fruit ripen faster...

if stored next to apples and tomatoes.

Apples, tomatoes and bananas all give off a gas called **ethylene** which makes some fruit and vegetables ripen faster. This can be helpful – but it can also mean that food can go bad before you get a chance to eat it.

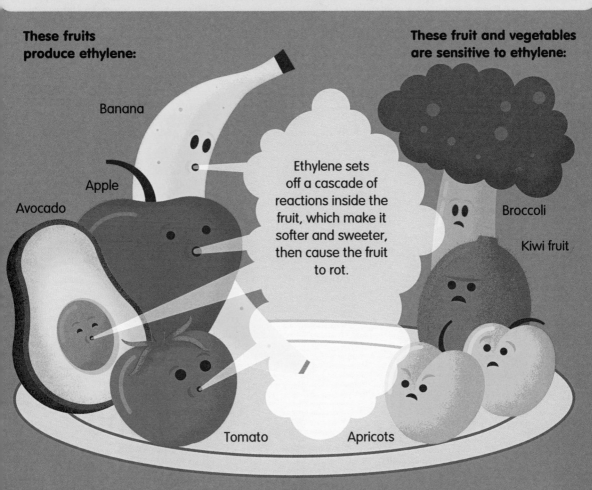

These fruits produce ethylene:

Banana

Apple

Avocado

Ethylene sets off a cascade of reactions inside the fruit, which make it softer and sweeter, then cause the fruit to rot.

These fruit and vegetables are sensitive to ethylene:

Broccoli

Kiwi fruit

Tomato

Apricots

Some fruit, such as bananas, produce ethylene *and* are sensitive to it.

So if you keep a banana by itself in a sealed bag, it will ripen all on its own.

49 There's a spice more expensive...
than silver and gold.

Saffron, a yellow spice derived from the stigmas inside crocus flowers, is the most expensive food in the world. By weight, it can even be more expensive than gold. The reason it costs so much is that it must be harvested by hand.

Stigma

Each crocus bulb only produces

1

flower.

Each flower produces just

3

stigmas, which are so delicate they must be harvested by hand.

The flower blooms only

1

time each year.

This is the actual size of a saffron crocus.

The stigmas are dried, and shrink to just

20%

of their original size.

Saffron has been used to flavor dishes for over

4,000

years.

This all means a farmer has to grow

150

flowers to produce *just*

1g (0.035oz)

of saffron.

1g of saffron can cost up to

$90

1g of gold costs about

$35

50 There are thousands of ways...

to make food taste like strawberry.

Chemists known as **flavorists** have the job of making thousands of new food flavorings using chemicals taken from just about everything.

Flavorists travel the world...

...extracting chemicals from plants and animals...

...sampling the best meals to see which flavors work well together...

...and exploring remote locations to bring back new flavors.

Then, in a lab, they combine chemicals to mimic the tastes of foods – and improve them.

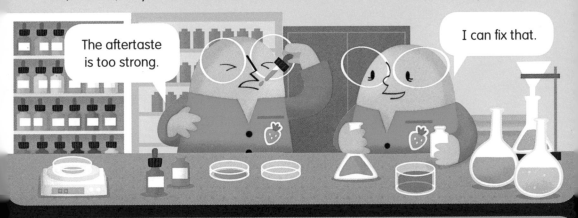

The aftertaste is too strong.

I can fix that.

They can create each flavor in thousands of ways – for example, some companies have designed over **2,000 different recipes** just for strawberry flavors.

Chewing gum

Sodas

Candy

Ice cream

Milkshakes

51 | Salt, heat and ice...

have been used for centuries to preserve food.

Food often goes bad because of **bacteria** – microscopic creatures that invade and digest it. People discovered this only recently, but for thousands of years they have used different methods to preserve their food.

A history of food preservation:

Freezing (as old as people)

HOW: People living in areas that had hot and cold seasons learned that storing meat and fish in winter ice made them last longer.
WHY: Bacteria can't grow at very low temperatures.

Pickling
(first documented in India)
HOW: People found that foods such as cucumbers were preserved if put in salty water.
WHY: The cucumbers and salty brine make an acid solution, which kills bacteria.

Curing
(first documented in Ancient Greece)
HOW: People rubbed salt into meat to keep it from going bad.
WHY: Bacteria need moisture to live. Salt draws water out of meat, so bacteria can't survive in it.

Pasteurizing
(France, 1850s)

French chemist Louis Pasteur proved that bacteria are the reason food goes bad. He also invented a new preservation method: *pasteurization*.

HOW: Milk or wine is heated to 140-158°F, then cooled down again.
WHY: This temperature is enough to kill off bacteria. Heating it much higher would spoil the taste.

Vacuum packing
(1960s)
HOW: Food is wrapped in plastic film, all the air is sucked out and the package is tightly sealed.
WHY: Without air, bacteria can't survive.

Today, supermarkets contain a wide range of foods preserved using all of these techniques.

52 Can openers were invented...
forty-eight years *after* the invention of cans.

Food was first canned in 1810, but can openers weren't invented until 1858. Before then, the easiest way to open a can was with a hammer and chisel.

53 Barbequed bluebottle...

tastes worse than mice on toast.

In the nineteenth century, an eccentric British geologist and paleontologist named William Buckland set himself the task of eating one of every creature in the animal kingdom – a practice known as **zoophagy**.

Here is a gallery of some of the unusual and exotic creatures that Buckland tried:

Mole

Insects

Rhino

Mouse

Elephant

Porpoise

Bluebottle

Buckland said bluebottle was the worst of all the foods he tried.

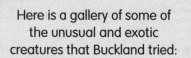

There are records of some of the ways he cooked and ate the animals he tried, including barbequed bluebottles, and rhino pie.

54 A termite burger...

has more protein than a beef burger.

Insects could be widely farmed as food in the future. They have high protein, fat and mineral content, and farming them has a less harmful impact on the environment than farming other animals.

Here's how much protein you'd get in 4 ounces of different types of burgers.

Cricket — 0.4 oz

Beef — 1 oz

Caterpillar — 1.1 oz

Termite — 1.2 oz

Insects can be ground up to make burgers. But, if you were feeling adventurous, you could follow one of these recipes.

Crickets
Serve roasted and with garlic, lime juice and salt.

Caterpillars
Boil in salted water and sun-dry before eating.

Termites
Sun-dry, smoke or steam in banana leaves.

are drunk every day.

Every day, people around the world drink three billion cups of tea – three times more than coffee. While all teas come from the leaves of one type of plant, they can be turned into hundreds of types of tea, drunk in a variety of ways.

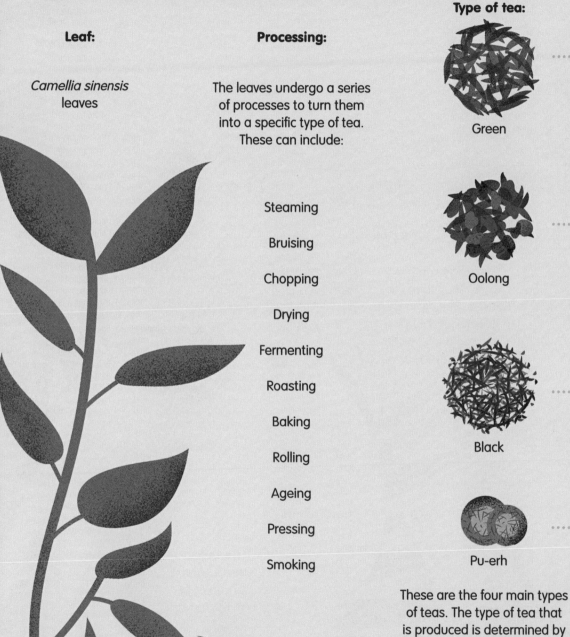

Type of tea:

Leaf:

Processing:

Camellia sinensis leaves

The leaves undergo a series of processes to turn them into a specific type of tea. These can include:

Green

Steaming

Bruising

Chopping

Oolong

Drying

Fermenting

Roasting

Baking

Black

Rolling

Ageing

Pressing

Smoking

Pu-erh

These are the four main types of teas. The type of tea that is produced is determined by which processes are used on the leaves.

The dry tea leaves are usually brewed in hot water, and then other things may be added. Here are some of the ways tea is drunk around the world:

Sugar
Mint leaves
Tea

Powdered tea

Japan

Morocco

Jasmine flowers
Tea

China

Toasted rice
Tea

Japan

Sugar
Milk
Tea
Tapioca

Taiwan

Tea

China

Smoked tea leaves
Tea

Russia

Spices
Salt
Milk
Tea

Pakistan

Sugar
Spices
Milk
Tea

India

Ice
Sugar
Tea

USA

Milk
Tea

UK & Ireland

Tea

Turkey

Salt
Yak butter
Tea

Tibet

Tea

China

More tea is drunk per person in Turkey than any other country, followed by Ireland and the UK.

67

56 You eat water...

as well as drinking it.

You need to take in water every day. It keeps your blood circulating, enables food to flow through your digestive system, and helps your joints move. But much of the water you consume comes from your food.

Here are the percentages of water found in some common foods and drinks:

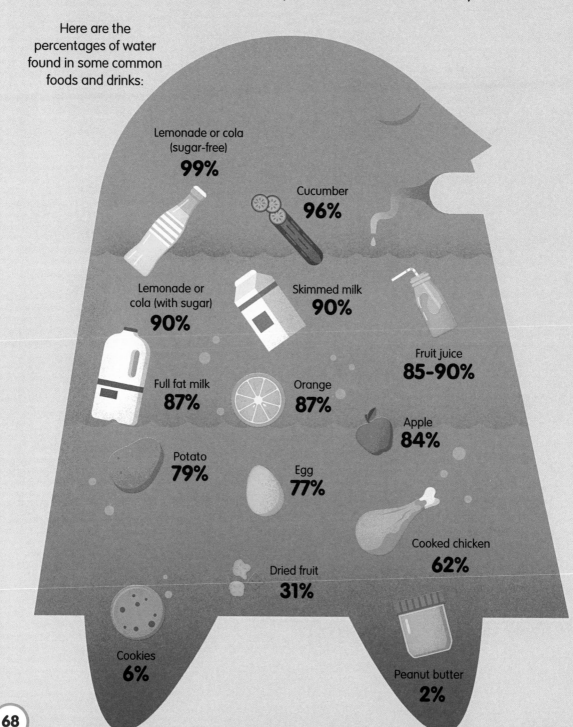

Lemonade or cola (sugar-free)
99%

Cucumber
96%

Lemonade or cola (with sugar)
90%

Skimmed milk
90%

Fruit juice
85-90%

Full fat milk
87%

Orange
87%

Apple
84%

Potato
79%

Egg
77%

Cooked chicken
62%

Dried fruit
31%

Cookies
6%

Peanut butter
2%

57 Honey lasts forever...

because it's a natural bacteria killer.

Pots of honey have been found in Ancient Egyptian tombs. Even though they were buried thousands of years ago, the honey's still edible. Honey lasts so long because bacteria, which make other foods go bad, can't survive in it.

Honey has **three properties** that make it antibacterial.

Honey is **hygroscopic,** which means that it contains very little water. Bacteria can't survive without water.

Honey is **acidic**. It contains gluconic acid which kills bacteria.

Honey contains a tiny amount of **hydrogen peroxide** – the stuff that bleach is often made from. This also kills bacteria.

58 Peanut butter gets stickier...

when you put it in your mouth.

When you eat, your mouth releases a liquid called **saliva**. It's 99% water, but saliva also contains enzymes that help you digest food.

Peanut butter draws in water from your saliva, turning hard and sticky.

Glands ····▶ where saliva is made

Arachibutyrophobics are people who are scared of peanut butter sticking to the roof of their mouth.

59 Bananas can stand in for eggs...

when you bake a cake.

Cakes are usually made from flour, sugar, eggs and fat (oil or butter) – but they don't have to be. You can often make a cake by trading one or two ingredients for foods that have similar properties, even if the cake tastes a little different.

Here are some alternative ingredients, if you don't have, or can't eat, the usual ones.

Flour adds form and structure to cakes.

Flour alternatives:

Black beans

Ground oats

Ground nuts

Sugar sweetens cakes and helps make them soft.

Sugar alternatives:

Honey

Agave nectar

Fruit purée

Eggs bind ingredients and give a fluffy texture.

Egg alternatives:

Prune purée

Mashed potato

Mashed banana

Fat helps make cakes fluffy and moist.

Fat alternatives:

Tofu

Mashed avocado

Plain yogurt

60 A car can be an oven...

when its engine is running.

You need heat to cook, but you don't always need an oven, stove or grill. Heat from any source will do, as long as the food gets hot enough for long enough.

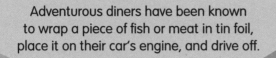

Adventurous diners have been known to wrap a piece of fish or meat in tin foil, place it on their car's engine, and drive off.

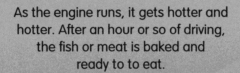

As the engine runs, it gets hotter and hotter. After an hour or so of driving, the fish or meat is baked and ready to to eat.

Firemen working on steam trains used to fry eggs and bacon on a shovel over the fire, as if it were a frying pan.

The engine of a nuclear submarine gets so hot that submariners have been known to bake potatoes on it.

61 From bean to bar...

making chocolate can be a tricky process.

It takes a series of careful steps to get from a cacao tree to a chocolate bar. Follow this flowchart to find out what is involved.

Key

- ⬭ Start/End
- ◆ Decision
- ▬ Action

START HERE

Cacao tree

Cocoa pods

Harvest green or orange pods?

Green pods aren't ripe. **START AGAIN!**

Orange pods are ripe. Scoop out **the beans** inside.

Ferment the beans for 3-8 days under banana leaves to develop their flavor.

Leave the beans alone or turn them regularly?

Undisturbed beans ferment unevenly. **START AGAIN!**

Turn the beans several times to ferment them evenly.

Dry the fermented beans to make them less acidic and bitter. Dry slowly, steadily or quickly?

If they dry too slowly they get moldy. **START AGAIN!**

Pick a steady drying method.

If they dry too quickly they stay bitter and acidic. **START AGAIN!**

Dry in the sun for a week.

Dry near a wood fire to give the chocolate a smoky flavor.

Bag the beans.

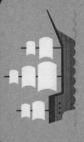

Transport the beans to a chocolate factory.

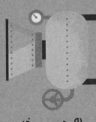

Roast the beans. The longer and hotter the roast, the more intense the flavor.

How hot?

Roast between 200 and 300°F.

Above 300°C, the beans will burn. **START AGAIN!**

Winnow the beans – remove the outer husks, leaving behind **cocoa nibs.**

Grind the cocoa nibs into a paste called **cocoa mass.**

Mix in sugar and other ingredients, such as milk.

Conch the mixture – gently beat it with metal beads. Conch for less than a day or up to three days?

Less than a day and the mixture will still be lumpy. **GO BACK A STEP.**

Conching for one to three days gives a smooth texture.

Temper the mixture – gradually heat it and cool it.

Above 115°F, the mixture becomes

Heating it up to 115°F makes it slick and shiny.

Pour the mixture into a mold.

At last, the chocolate

All foods are radioactive...

especially brazil nuts.

All foods are slightly radioactive, because elements such as potassium and radium, which can be radioactive, occur naturally in soil. These are transferred into plants as they grow.

Radioactivity in food is measured in units called **picocuries**.
1 brazil nut contains about **30 picocuries** of radiation.

To get the same amount of radiation as one brazil nut from each of the *next* most radioactive foods, you'd have to eat:

250
carrots
= 30 picocuries

110
potatoes
= 30 picocuries

275
bananas
= 30 picocuries

A truck full of bananas is radioactive enough to set off alarms at ports, designed to detect nuclear smuggling.

But you'd have to eat over
10 million
bananas to get radiation poisoning.

63 You can't make gelatin dessert...

with kiwi fruit.

Gelatin is a substance made up of tangled strands of protein. But fresh fruit such as kiwis, pineapples and papayas contain protein-digesting enzymes, and this will stop the dessert from setting.

When you add hot water to gelatin, its strands of proteins separate.

As it cools, the strands tangle up again and the gelatin sets. Most fruit won't prevent this.

Wobble

Wobble

Wobble

Pull yourself together!

But if you add kiwi fruit, its enzymes break down the strands into shorter sections.

The dessert cools, the strands are now too short to recombine, so the gelatin won't set.

64 Too many carrots...

will make your skin orange.

A carrot's orange color is caused by a chemical called **beta-carotene**. If you eat a lot of carrots, carotene can build up in your blood and temporarily turn your skin yellow.

This is a harmless condition called **carotenosis**.

It is quite common in babies and children who have been fed a lot of carrots.

65 Hot chili peppers can kill...

by triggering heart attacks and seizures.

What makes chilis hot is a chemical called **capsaicin**. Eating an enormous amount of capsaicin at once can send your body into shock.

The heat of a chili can be measured in units called **Scoville Heat Units (SHUs)** on the **Scoville scale**.

15,000,000–16,000,000
Pure capsaicin: colorless, odorless and potentially deadly.

2,000,000–5,300,000
Pepper spray: used as a weapon, and may cause temporary blindness.

855,000–2,199,999
Bhut jolokia (also known as the *ghost pepper*)

100,000–350,000
Habanero

100,000–200,000
Scotch bonnet

SHUs are measured by extracting capsaicin from dried peppers – which are far hotter than fresh peppers.

If you eat a very hot pepper, it's better to cool your mouth down by drinking *milk*, rather than water. Milk helps wash the capsaicin away, but water can't do that.

10,000–23,000
Cayenne

2,500–5,000
Jalapeño

0
Bell pepper: no heat

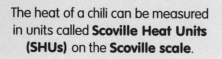

Dried, moldy, fermented fish...
the savory secret behind Japanese cuisine.

hundreds of years, Japanese chefs have used an ingredient called
suobushi to give their dishes a rich umami flavor. Katsuobushi is made
m tuna in a process that can take up to a year to complete.

2

Cut whole skipjack tuna fish (*Katsuwonus pelamis*) into four large fillets.

Simmer them in water for about two hours, then clean and debone them.

For roughly one month, alternate between smoking and air-drying the fillets.

Finally, shave the katsuobushi into thin, rosy flakes and use them in stocks and sauces, or as a savory topping for rice dishes, noodles and even pizza.

Coat them with a mold called *Aspergillus glaucus* and lay them out to dry.

As the mold ferments, it devours fat and moisture, drying the fish even more.

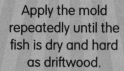

Apply the mold repeatedly until the fish is dry and hard as driftwood.

67 Jamaica's national fruit...

contains a deadly poison.

Eating *some parts* of an ackee fruit, the national fruit of Jamaica, can cause fatal illness. Yet ackee is an essential ingredient in traditional Jamaican cooking. Here are some of the world's most deadly foods.

Ackee fruit

Toxin: Hypoglycin
Found in: Unripe ackee fruit; seeds
Can cause: Jamaican Vomiting Sickness; coma; death

Eaten in: Jamaica
Preparation: The mature fruit breaks open naturally, exposing ripe flesh, which is safe to eat once the toxic black seeds have been removed.
Typical dish: Ackee and saltfish

POLICE DEPARTMENT
ACKEE FRUIT

ARRESTED

Fugu (pufferfish)

Toxin: Tetrodotoxin
Found in: Fugu livers, eyes, intestines and other organs
Can cause: Numbness; paralysis; death

Eaten in: Japan
Preparation: Specially trained and licensed chefs cut up the fugu and separate out all the poisonous parts.
Typical dish: Fugu sashimi (raw fugu sliced paper-thin)

POLICE DEPARTMENT
FUGU
(PUFFERFISH)

ARRESTED

A single fugu contains enough tetrodotoxin to kill **30 people**.

It is so dangerous that, for his own safety, the Japanese emperor is forbidden by law to eat fugu.

Cashew nuts

Toxin: Anacardic acid
Found in: The shells around raw cashew 'nuts' (which are actually seeds)
Can cause: Severe skin irritation and burns; death if swallowed or inhaled

Eaten: Worldwide
Preparation: Roasting cashew nuts destroys the toxin.
Typical dish: Chicken and cashew

Cassava root

Toxin: Cyanide
Found in: Raw or unprocessed cassava root
Can cause: Vertigo; vomiting; nerve damage; paralysis; death

Eaten in: Africa, Asia, South America, the Caribbean
Preparation: Cassava root can be ground into flour and processed with a combination of soaking, drying, fermenting and cooking.
Typical dish: Tapioca pudding

Rhubarb

Toxin: Oxalic acid
Found in: Rhubarb leaves
Can cause: Burning sensation; inflammation; joint pain; kidney failure; death

Eaten: Worldwide
Preparation: The leaves are discarded; only the stalks are edible.
Typical dish: Rhubarb crumble

68 Top restaurant critics...

lead secret lives.

The most admired award in the restaurant business is called a **Michelin Star**. There is often a media frenzy surrounding the awarding of Stars, but the critics who decide which restaurants deserve them remain completely anonymous.

Michelin critics visit secretly, to make sure standards are consistently high.

Any one of the diners in this restaurant could be a Michelin critic...

Some Michelin-starred restaurants have as many staff as there are customers.

Food must be extremely fresh.

Critics never reveal why a star was given...

...or taken away.

Stars are awarded one at a time, up to a maximum of three stars.

Only around 100 restaurants in the whole world have three Michelin Stars. That's about one in every 150,000 restaurants.

69 Michelin Stars...

were invented to sell cars.

The Michelin Star system was started by French brothers who ran a car tire company. In 1900, they published a guide to the roads, gas stations and restaurants of France, to encourage people to take up driving.

The guide suggested motorists visit certain restaurants:

1 Star – "a very good restaurant"

2 Stars – "worth a detour"

3 Stars – "worth a special journey"

Over the last 100 years, the star has turned into the most acclaimed accolade for a chef, anywhere in the world.

70 Most bananas are clones...

and could be wiped out with one disease.

There are over 1,000 varieties of bananas, but only one variety, **Cavendish**, is transported and sold in stores overseas. Every Cavendish banana is a clone – that means they all have exactly the same genes.

Cloned Cavendish bananas are **sterile**, which means they can't reproduce. They're all grown from the roots of existing plants, and are all identical.

As all Cavendish bananas have the **same genes**, an infection in one plant could quickly spread...

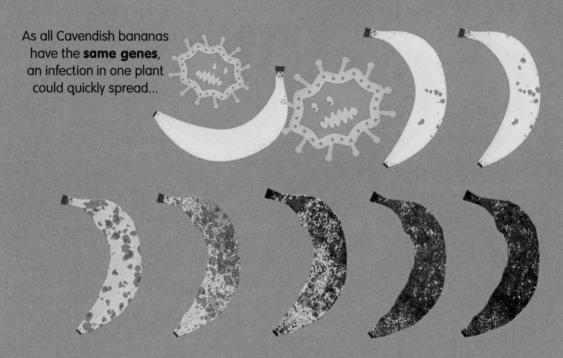

...and cause them all to perish.

In case that happens, scientists are working on developing a new variety that's tasty, transportable, and resistant to diseases.

71 A cloud of flour...

could blow up a bread factory.

Flour, an ingredient used all around the world every day to make bread, is highly explosive. If a cloud of flour dust is suspended in the air, even a tiny spark could trigger an explosion powerful enough blow up an entire building. Here's how it works.

1 A spark ignites one grain of flour, which burns.

2 Oxygen in the air keeps the grain burning long enough to ignite more nearby grains.

3 A chain reaction is triggered, igniting all the grains.

4 The flour-filled air explodes.

Why is a cloud of flour so explosive?

Flour is a **carbohydrate**, made of long chains of **sugar**. Sugar is a highly flammable substance that burns very quickly.

Sugar

Because flour is a powder, it can spread out in a tight space, and mix with oxygen in the air. The oxygen is what makes the flour burn.

72 Hating Brussels sprouts...
might be in your DNA.

Your DNA, the chemical code that makes you you, gives you a specific set of taste receptors on your tongue. Some people's receptors are very sensitive to certain chemicals, causing an unavoidable dislike of particular foods.

40%
of people dislike truffles.

Truffles, a delicacy similar to mushrooms, are full of a chemical called **androstenone**. 40% of people are very sensitive to androstenone, and find it tastes and smells like stale sweat.

10%
of people dislike cilantro.

A version of a receptor called **OR6A2** makes one in ten people sensitive to chemicals called **aldehydes**. To them, cilantro tastes like soap.

50%
of people dislike sprouts.

About half the population has a version of a receptor called **TAS2R38**. This makes certain chemicals found in sprouts and broccoli taste bitter and unpleasant.

It's a coincidence that the percentages on this page add up to 100%. You might like or hate some of these foods, or all three of them.

73 Valuable fungi...

are hunted by pigs.

Truffles are a kind of edible fungus that grows underground in woodlands. This makes them hard for people to find without the help of specially trained pigs to help sniff them out.

Truffles are most often found at the bases of beech, birch, oak, pine and fir trees.

Truffles produce a smell similar to that of **androstenol** – a chemical produced by male pigs that attracts female pigs.

In some countries, dogs are used instead of pigs, as truffles smell so delicious to pigs that they tend to eat them.

Truffles

Truffles are very expensive, because they are so hard to find. In 2010, a truffle the size of a football sold for over $300,000.

74 The smell of bacon...

has saved lives.

Bacon has such an enticing smell that police detectives have actually used it to lure kidnappers out of hiding, so people they have taken hostage can be rescued.

Early one morning in a bustling metropolis...

...a criminal is up to no good.

Don't move!

How could we?

Come out with your hands up.

No way! If you come in, someone's gonna get it!

Let's wait him out.

Uniformed officer

Negotiator

Why does bacon smell so good?

Some chemicals travel through the air, and can be detected when they enter our noses. They are known as **aroma compounds**.

1
Bacon contains sugar and protein, which is made up of smaller molecules called amino acids. When cooked, the sugar and amino acids react together, forming a range of aroma compounds.

This is called the **Maillard Reaction**.

He must be tired and hungry by now. I know how to coax him out.

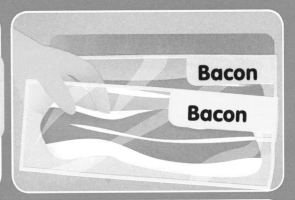

Bacon

Bacon

Mmm, smells delicious.

We're having breakfast out here. You should join us.

I'm so hungry, I can't take it anymore.

OK, OK, I'm coming out.

This tactic really has been used by police negotiators.

2 Even more aroma compounds are created when fat in the bacon melts and reacts with nitrates that are added to the bacon to preserve it.

3 The sheer number and variety of aroma compounds, and their endless combinations, make bacon smell delicious to many people.

75 Electric drinks...

keep athletes going for longer.

Long-distance runners use up lots of energy as they race, and they sweat out water and important minerals. Many sip sports drinks along the way, to help them reach the finish line.

Long-distance runners burn up lots of energy. If they don't replenish that energy, they might not finish their race.

Losing too much water can lead to headaches, nausea, fatigue and muscle cramps.

So... tired...

Sweating keeps athletes cool – but uses up water and minerals called **electrolytes**.

Aah! My calves are cramping up!

76 Every olive counts...

at cruising altitude.

Every day, nearly 10 million people around the world board airplanes. It takes careful planning and hard work to feed all those passengers safely, efficiently and, from the airline's point of view, economically.

$4-5
is the maximum desired cost of one in-flight meal. To stick to it, airlines plan their menus a year in advance.

10 hours
is the average time between meals being made and meals being heated up to be served during a flight.

FINISH

Woohoo!

Electrolytes form electrically charged particles in the blood. Muscles need these in order to work properly.

Sports drinks contain water, electrolytes and sugar, for energy – all designed to help athletes succeed.

35,000ft up
at cruising altitude, air pressure is low. Recipes are tested in low-pressure chambers to see how they'll taste on board.

30% of sensitivity
to sweet and salt is lost as air pressure drops. Food is designed to taste good despite passengers' diminished sense of taste.

$40,000 per year
is the amount one US airline saved in the 1980s, by removing just **one olive** from each salad served in first class.

77 Friendly vegetables...

protect and support each other.

Thousands of years ago, Native Americans lived mainly on three crops: squash, corn and beans. These grew best when planted together. This technique – called **companion planting** – is still used in small-scale farming, for a variety of crop combinations.

The tall corn plants support the beans as they grow, enabling them to get as much sunlight as possible.

Prickles on the squash leaves and stems stop animals, such as raccoons, from eating the crops.

Beans ·······▸

Corn ·······▸

Big, flat squash leaves shelter the soil and keep it moist.

Squash

Moisture is drawn up by the plants' roots and helps them to thrive.

Bacteria living in the beans' roots release useful substances called **nitrates** into the soil, which the corn and squash need to grow.

Nitrates

A fungal disease...

makes corn more nutritious.

Huitlacoche (pronounced weet-la-KOH-chay), or 'corn smut', is a gray fungus that grows on corn. It also changes the chemical make-up of the corn itself, so that it contains more nutrients than uninfected corn.

Huitlacoche contains high levels of two nutrients known as **lysine** and **beta-glucans**.

Lysine

This is a chemical we need in our diets to help fight infections and strengthen our bones.

Beta-glucans

This is soluble **fiber** that helps lower **cholesterol** – a fatty substance that's thought to contribute to heart disease.

Huitlacoche tastes like a cross between mushrooms and corn.

In many parts of the world, corn infected with huitlacoche is thrown away. But it's a delicacy in some countries, such as Mexico, where many farmers infect their corn with the disease on purpose.

79 Champagne isn't champagne...

unless it's made in Champagne.

People have long understood that *where* a food is produced has a major effect on how it tastes. The Champagne region of France, for example, is famous for its fine sparkling wine. It is considered so special that, under French law, only sparkling wine produced there can be called 'champagne'.

Winemakers can produce sparkling wine anywhere. But what makes champagne unique is its particular **terroir** – the combination of local factors that may determine how the grapes develop and how the wine will taste:

Local weather conditions: temperature, rainfall, number of days of sunshine per year

Champagne

Picardie

Champagne

Sparkling wine

In order to promote the country's culinary heritage and maintain a rich variety of foods, French laws recognize and protect hundreds of different products with their own particular terroirs. These include:

Lamb from the salt marshes of the Somme river

Butter from Poitou-Charente

Cheese from Roquefort-sur-Soulzon

Honey from Corsica

Lentils from Le Puy-en-Velay

Lavender oil from Provence

The shape of the landscape: steep and hilly or flat and shady, in a valley or on a plain, facing north or facing south

The type of soil: rocky, chalky, or loamy, fast-draining or damp

Local growing methods and winemaking traditions: the tools, timing and expertise used in pruning, irrigating and harvesting

80 Insect-nibbled tea leaves...

are the ones to pick.

Dong Fang Mei Ren, or *Oriental Beauty*, is one of the world's most valued oolong teas. It has sweet, citrusy flavors that have an unlikely source: the tiny bites made by a marauding insect.

For a few weeks every summer, an insect called the **tea jassid** descends on Taiwanese tea plantations to feed.

Tea plant
Scientific name:
Camellia sinensis

Tea jassid
Scientific name:
Jacobiasca formosana

Nibbled leaves release chemicals called **terpenes**, which help the leaves recover and discourage the jassids from further attack.

These terpenes are fragrant too, and change the taste of the leaves.

Tea farmers pluck only the damaged leaves. This helps ensure the resulting tea has a distinct and concentrated flavor.

81 Smoked eel and chocolate...

should taste great together.

Foods contain different chemical compounds that give them their unique flavors. Some chefs believe that by combining foods that share many of the same compounds they can make tasty new dishes.

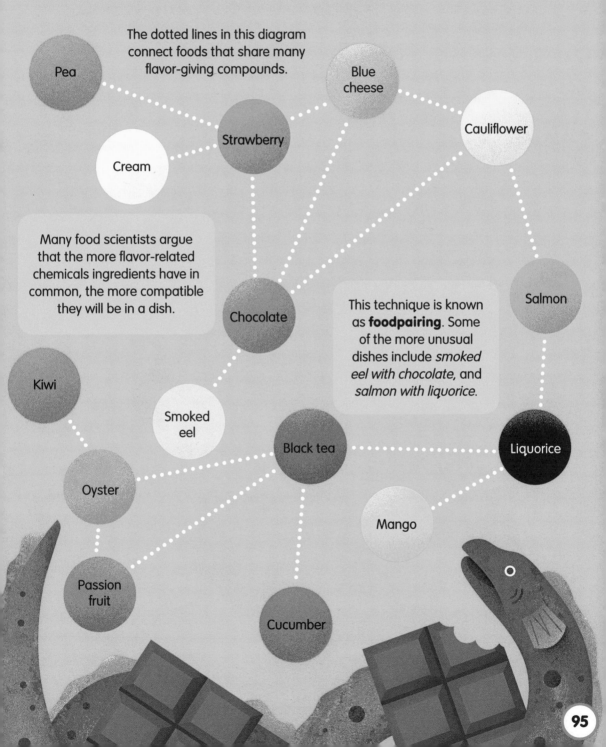

The dotted lines in this diagram connect foods that share many flavor-giving compounds.

Pea

Blue cheese

Cauliflower

Strawberry

Cream

Many food scientists argue that the more flavor-related chemicals ingredients have in common, the more compatible they will be in a dish.

Chocolate

Salmon

This technique is known as **foodpairing**. Some of the more unusual dishes include *smoked eel with chocolate,* and *salmon with liquorice.*

Kiwi

Smoked eel

Black tea

Liquorice

Oyster

Mango

Passion fruit

Cucumber

You couldn't make a burrito...

before the year 1492.

Many of the ingredients found in our kitchen pantries originated on separate continents. It wasn't until the explorer Christopher Columbus sailed from Europe to Central America in 1492 that ships began regularly crossing the Atlantic – and some of the world's favorite foods became possible.

A burrito is a popular Mexican dish. It combines various ingredients – originally from separate sides of the Atlantic – wrapped in a flour tortilla.

Originally from Europe and Asia

Originally from America

Bell peppers and chili peppers

When Columbus arrived in America, he had never before seen foods such as peppers, tomatoes or beans.

Tomatoes and avocados

Corn and beans

Chicken, pork and beef

Cheese and sour cream

The Native Americans Columbus met encountered many foods for the first time, too.

Cilantro, rice and lime

In the centuries since Columbus's voyage, dozens of plants and animals have been traded between the continents. This process is called the **Columbian Exchange**.

- pasta
- tomato
- olive oil
- basil

- bread
- beef
- tomato
- potato

- cacao beans
- milk
- sugar

Chefs combined these ingredients in new ways, creating many of the foods we eat today.

Spaghetti & tomato sauce

Burger & fries

Hot chocolate

83 Potatoes and wood chips...

lifted spirits during the Second World War.

During the War (1939 to 1945), ships carrying food to Britain were blockaded, so lots of ingredients were in short supply. To make sure food was distributed fairly, **rationing** was introduced. This meant everyone was only entitled to a limited amount of food.

To keep public morale high, the government came up with some creative recipes to make a variety of dishes, often using some surprising ingredients.

'Mock apricot tart'

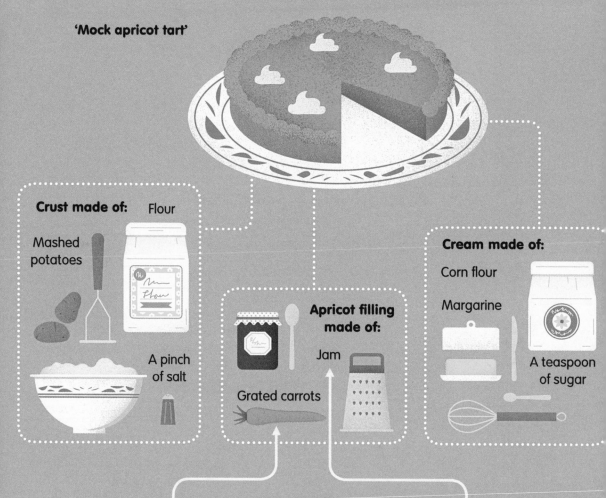

Crust made of: Flour

Mashed potatoes

A pinch of salt

Apricot filling made of:

Jam

Grated carrots

Cream made of:

Corn flour

Margarine

A teaspoon of sugar

There wasn't much sugar around. Children were given carrots on sticks instead of lollipops, and there was even a soft drink made of carrot and swede, called *carrolade*.

Sometimes tiny wood chips were added to jam to look like raspberry seeds, which made the jam seem more full of fruit.

84 A mud pie...

could be a healthy snack.

Eating mud could provide people with useful nutrients and protect them from harmful toxins – but only if they ate the *right* mud.

I boiled the mud first, so it should be safe to eat.

Since I've been pregnant, I've been craving mud. Scientists think it may help soothe my morning sickness.

Topsoils are dangerous to eat, as they are full of parasites, pollutants and pesticides.

Some soil from lower down, however, could contain nutritious minerals, such as:

Magnesium   **Calcium**   **Iron**   **Copper**

Clay

Types of soil containing clay may create a protective barrier in the gut that absorbs toxins and harmful bacteria.

White clay

Eating *too much* mud can cause constipation, though. Doctors have tried to use this effect in a beneficial way by adding white clay to anti-diarrhea medicines.

85 Dill is the mirror image...

of spearmint, at a molecular level.

Spearmint and dill are two green leafy herbs that have very different flavors. Yet it's the same chemical, **carvone**, that makes them both taste the way they do. What makes them different is how the carvone molecules are arranged.

Carvone molecules can be arranged in two different ways that are mirror images of each other – like left and right hands.

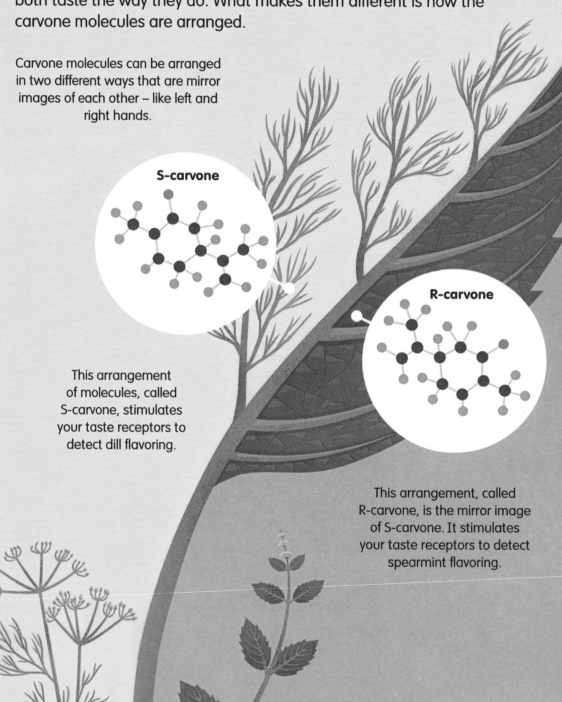

S-carvone

R-carvone

This arrangement of molecules, called S-carvone, stimulates your taste receptors to detect dill flavoring.

This arrangement, called R-carvone, is the mirror image of S-carvone. It stimulates your taste receptors to detect spearmint flavoring.

86 A lick of ice cream...

could cost you your life.

In the 19th century, in cities such as London, ice cream was sold in tiny glasses that were licked clean, then reused by vendors. Eventually this practice was linked to the spread of a deadly lung disease, called **tuberculosis**.

Ice cream was sold in glasses known as 'penny licks', although they actually came in a range of prices.

The ice cream was licked out and the glass was reused without being washed.

Halfpenny

Penny

Tuppence

1899

Penny licks were banned in London in an attempt to stop the spread of tuberculosis...

...which was passed through saliva...

...from person... ...to person.

1904

Vendors experimented with new ways of serving ice cream.

Many tried out various edible ice cream cups.

When the waffle cone was invented it quickly became the standard method for selling ice cream.

87 Whale goo...

was once used to flavor ice cream.

The earliest known recipe for ice cream, dating to the 1660s, includes **ambergris** – a rare, waxy substance made by sperm whales, found floating in the sea. Over time, ambergris develops a long-lasting sweet odor.

Ambergris is just one example of animal goo used in cooking...

Cochineal

Made from: crushed cochineal beetles – a type of bug that lives on cacti in South and Central America

Use: bright red food dye

Castoreum

Made from: a fluid secreted from beavers' glands.

Use: vanilla flavorings for foods including ice cream

Gelatin

Made from: boiled up animal bones and skin

Use: to set desserts such as jelly and mousses

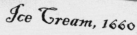

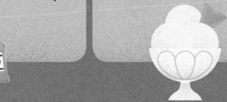

Lanolin

Made from: greasy oil found in sheep's wool

Use: to makes some foods look shiny. Also used in chewing gum.

GUM

Shellac

Made from: a thick, sticky substance excreted by lac bugs

Use: shiny candy shells, a coating for citrus fruits to make them last longer

Ice Cream, 1660

Take three pints of the best cream, boyle it with mace, or else flavor it with orange flower water or ambergris...

88 Vegetables self-destruct...
when they reach the end of their shelf lives.

The period of time when food is in good condition or safe to eat is known as its **shelf life**. Any food's shelf life ends when it spoils, sometimes becoming dangerous to eat. But not all foods spoil in the same way.

Microbial spoilage
Bacteria, yeasts and molds feed off moisture and nutrients in food, multiplying and making it bad to eat.

Yeasts spoil sugary foods, such as fruit.

Bacteria cause milk to curdle.

Bread is too dry for bacteria, but not for mold.

Bacteria that make people sick thrive in old meat and eggs.

Rancidification
Oxygen in the air breaks down fats in foods, making them turn rancid.

Fatty foods such as butter and peanut butter go rancid. They're not harmful to eat, but they taste unpleasant.

Autolysis (self-destruction)
Many natural foods contain molecules called **enzymes** that cause them to change or decay by themselves.

Autolysis can cause the protective skins of fruit and vegetables to rot, letting in mold and bacteria.

89 You can grow tomatoes in space...

without any soil.

Growing food during long, long voyages, sounds like a great idea – but it's a challenge to stop soil from floating around in a spacecraft. US space agency NASA is looking into **hydroponics,** a type of farming already used on Earth, where plants are grown only in water.

Here's a simplified version of how hydroponic systems work:

Nutrients – chemicals such as potassium, nitrogen and phosphorus – are added to the water to help the plants grow.

In space, the plant pots would be strapped down, and tightly covered, to make sure nothing could escape.

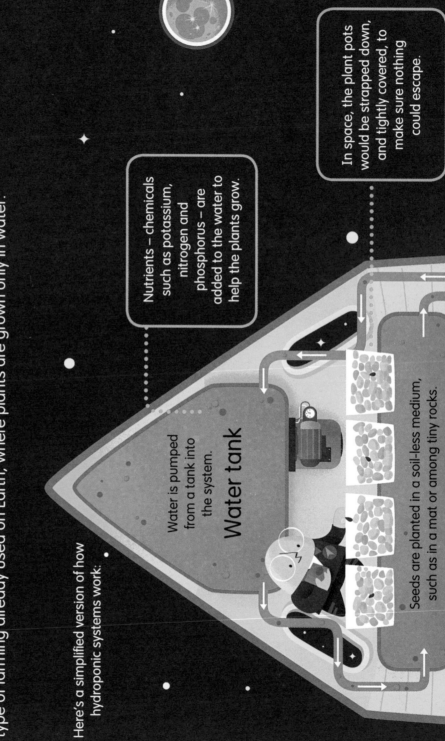

Water is pumped from a tank into the system.

Water tank

Seeds are planted in a soil-less medium, such as in a mat or among tiny rocks.

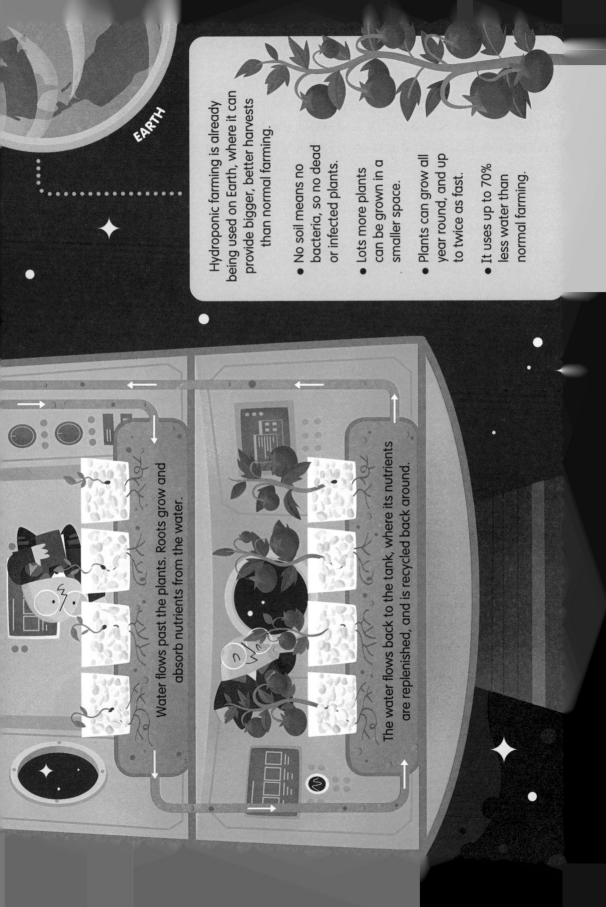

EARTH

Hydroponic farming is already being used on Earth, where it can provide bigger, better harvests than normal farming.

- No soil means no bacteria, so no dead or infected plants.

- Lots more plants can be grown in a smaller space.

- Plants can grow all year round, and up to twice as fast.

- It uses up to 70% less water than normal farming.

Water flows past the plants. Roots grow and absorb nutrients from the water.

The water flows back to the tank, where its nutrients are replenished, and is recycled back around.

90 Motor oil and lipstick...

help sell steaks and strawberries.

We are surrounded by images of food – in magazines, on billboards, and in television advertisements. But while the images may *look* appetizing, the foods depicted in them aren't always edible. Or even actually food.

Most foods don't hold up well in the hot lights and long hours of a photo shoot or filming session. Bubbles burst. Ice cream melts. Meat dries out.

So some professional **food stylists** use a range of materials and techniques that, while making the dishes inedible, also make them look amazing.

"Ice cream" made from lard, powdered sugar, and food coloring

Strawberries reddened with lipstick

Clear plastic or acrylic cubes

Bubbles made by a hidden fizzy tablet

Condensation effect made using spray-on deodorant

Grill marks applied with a branding iron

Basted with motor oil for shine and color

Seared on the outside with a blowtorch – raw on the inside

Soap foam

White glue

Diluted soy sauce

Sesame seeds placed with tweezers and stuck on with glue

Fries are individually selected and artfully arranged

Layers of toppings held in place with hidden toothpicks and cardboard spacers

Lettuce sprayed with glycerin for a crisp, glossy look

Cheese melted onto cold meat with a hairdryer

91 Coffee doesn't wake you up...

it keeps you from feeling sleepy.

A Chemicals called **adenosines** occur naturally in our bodies.

A They bind with receptors in our brains, sending chemical messages through our bodies that make us feel sleepy.

C Coffee contains a chemical called **caffeine**, which has a similar structure to adenosines.

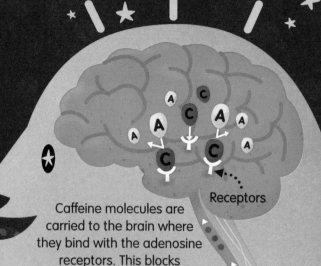

Caffeine molecules are carried to the brain where they bind with the adenosine receptors. This blocks messages from adenosines, so you stay alert.

Receptors

92 Green potatoes make you sick...

but not because they're green.

If potatoes are exposed to light and heat, they produce **chlorophyll** – the same chemical that makes leaves green – which is harmless to eat.

But light also makes potatoes produce large amounts of **solanine**. This can cause nausea, stomach cramps and dizziness.

If a potato is green, it's a good indicator that it's also poisonous.

93 Breadfruit...

could help feed the world.

A ninth of the people in the world do not have **food security**, which means they do not reliably have enough food to eat every day. There's no simple answer, but some scientists think breadfruit, originally grown in the South Pacific, could help.

Full of energy
Breadfruit are high in calories. Just one fruit contains enough carbohydrates to make a meal for a whole family.

Packed with protein
In areas where hunger is a problem, getting enough protein is often difficult. There's more protein in breadfruit than in other carbohydrate sources.

Rich in minerals
Breadfruit contains antioxidants, potassium, magnesium, iron, and lots of other crucial minerals.

Fights infection
Breadfruit contains high levels of vitamin C, a vitamin which protects you from illnesses.

Great grower
Breadfruit trees are easy and quick to grow, and they grow well in hot tropical countries, where food security can be a problem. Just one tree can produce over 200 fruits a year.

SERVING SUGGESTIONS:

Eat fresh and raw

Grind into flour

Cut into chunks to add to stews

Fry like french fries

Dry seeds to eat like nuts

Feels like bread, tastes like potato!

94 The ancient Maya ate...

their money.

Throughout history and around the world, certain foods have been used as money. What makes for a good edible currency? It should be portable, durable, standardized and, ideally, delicious.

Here are a few examples.

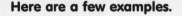

Cacao beans
Used by the ancient Maya in Central America
Prehistory – 17th century

Packs of mackerel snacks
Used by inmates in U.S. prisons
2004 – present day

Bars of rock salt
Used in Ethiopia
16th century – 20th century

Yams
Used by the basketful in the Pacific Ocean's Trobriand Islands
Prehistory – present day

Bricks of compressed tea
Used throughout Asia from Tibet to Siberia
Prehistory – 20th century

95 A single knife...

is all you need to prepare a Chinese banquet.

Chefs around the world use dozens of specialized kitchen knives – from flexible fish-filleting blades and long carving knives, to stubby peeling knives. Most Chinese chefs, however, rely on just one knife: the cleaver-like *tou*.

The flat side of the blade can be used to crush garlic or ginger.

The point of the blade can be used for precise and delicate cutting.

The edge of the blade can be used for chopping, slicing and scraping.

The spine of the blade can be used to make meat more tender by bashing it.

The flat side of the blade can also be used to scoop up and carry ingredients to the pan.

The butt of the handle can be used to crush or grind spices.

Knife skills are so central to classic Chinese cuisine that one Chinese term for cooking actually translates as 'to cut and cook'.

割烹

96 The last meal served on *Titanic*...
was a ten-course banquet.

On April 10th 1912 the biggest and most luxurious ship on the seas, the *Titanic*, set sail from England, bound for America. Part of the attraction of the voyage was the exclusive dining experience offered on board.

Four days after it set sail, disaster struck and *Titanic* sank.

Menus from the night it sank have been recovered, which give a glimpse into the luxury of life on-board.

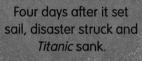

R.M.S. TITANIC

First-Class Menu

First course : Hors d'oeuvres – Oysters
Second course : Consommé 'Olga'
Third course : Salmon and cucumbers
Fourth course : Fillet steak 'Lili'
Fifth course : Lamb – Duckling – Beef sirloin
Sixth course : 'Punch Romaine'
Seventh course : Roast pigeon and cress
Eighth course : Cold asparagus vinaigrette
Ninth course : Foie gras pâté and celery
Tenth course : Peaches – Chocolate éclairs

. . . Tea and coffee . . .

. . . Wine, sherry and cigars . . .

The Titanic carried over **127,000** pieces of tableware: plates, glasses and silverware.

97 Farmers rent bees...

to keep fruit bowls filled.

To make fruit, many plants need a powder called **pollen** to be transferred from one flower to another, and bees help with this. When there are too few wild bees, farmers rent bee colonies to spread pollen around their crops.

A rental bee colony arrives when fruit trees are in blossom.

A bee lands on a flower to feed on nectar. Grains of pollen attach to its furry body.

The bee drops the pollen on the next flower that it visits.

The pollen makes the middle of the flower turn into a tiny new fruit and the petals fall away.

Over time, the fruit grows bigger and sweeter.

Bees roam up to 3km (2 miles) from their colony each day, then return at night.

A bee doesn't know where one farm starts and another stops, so farmers nearby benefit, too.

Rental bees are transported at night, because they don't move when it's dark so are less likely to get hurt on the journey.

To produce as much fruit as possible, an apple farmer would need

40,000 bees

for every 1 acre (0.4 hectares) of apple trees.

A French man named Michel Lotito became famous for eating metal and glass, and was known as *Monsieur Mangetout* (Mr. Eat-All). He ate 1kg (2.2lbs) of metal every day, and between 1978 and 1980 he managed to eat an entire plane.

Here are some of the objects he consumed over the course of his life.

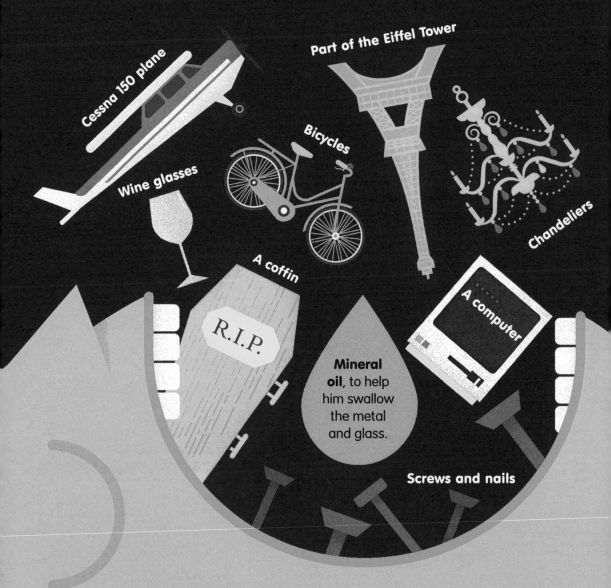

Cessna 150 plane

Part of the Eiffel Tower

Bicycles

Chandeliers

Wine glasses

A coffin

R.I.P.

A computer

Mineral **oil**, to help him swallow the metal and glass.

Screws and nails

Lotito was diagnosed with a condition called **pica**, which meant he wanted to eat things with no nutritional value. He also had a very thick stomach lining, which is how he could eat glass without cutting his insides.

99 Baking meringues on rainy days...

is a recipe for disaster.

Baked meringues are prepared by whisking egg whites with sugar. One of the most important parts of the recipe is keeping the ingredients as dry as possible. But on rainy or humid days, the sugar can absorb water from the air around it, altering the meringue mix.

If you follow a recipe from a book, your meringues should come out right.

Most recipe books tell cooks to make sure the mixing bowl is clean and dry.

Meringues

4 large egg whites

200g (1 cup) sugar

Whisk the egg whites first, then gradually add the sugar and whisk until the mixture forms stiff peaks.

Bake at 100°C (210°F) for 1½ hours

Whisking the mixture fills it with air – but this can be very tricky if the mixture becomes moist.

And you'll probably need to bake the meringues for longer than the recipe says – otherwise your meringues may not look or taste their best.

actually makes you sleepy.

Milk contains a chemical called **tryptophan**. Inside your body, tryptophan can be turned into messengers called hormones that help you sleep. Cows milked at night have more tryptophan in their milk.

Tryptophan
A chemical that can be turned into:

Serotonin
A 'happy' chemical in your brain, that helps make you feel relaxed and comfortable.

Melatonin
A chemical that helps regulate the body's sleep cycle. More is produced when it's dark.

At night, when cows should be sleeping, they have higher levels of tryptophan in their milk.

YAWN!

After drinking milk from a sleepy cow, serotonin and melatonin prepare you for sleep, slowing your body down and making you tired and relaxed.

Melatonin can make you so sleepy it is used to treat **insomnia** (not being able to sleep).

Glossary of food words

The glossary on the following four pages explains some of the words used in this book. Words in *italic* type have their own entries in the list.

agriculture The science of farming *crops* and *livestock*.

bacteria Microscopic organisms found in food and in your body. Many are good for you but some can cause illnesses.

bitter One of the five main *tastes*. Bitterness can indicate that a food is **toxic**, and prevent you from eating something harmful.

calories Units used to measure *energy* in food. One calorie is the amount of energy it takes to heat 1ml of water by 1°C.

carbohydrates A *food group*. Carbohydrates are made up of chains of *sugars*, and are important sources of *energy*.

cholesterol A compound found in most animal body tissues, which is essential to life but can be dangerous at high levels.

chefs Qualified, professional *cooks*.

clones Living things genetically identical to one another.

cook (1) To prepare food to eat by heating it. (2) Someone who prepares food, but not professionally.

crops Plants grown and harvested on a large scale for people to eat, particularly *grains*, *fruit* and *vegetables*.

dairy A *food group* that includes foods such as cheese and yogurt, all made from the milk of animals.

diet (1) The foods that a person eats. (2) If a person 'goes on a diet' he or she eats a restricted set of foods, to lose weight or to fit around a medical condition.

digesting Processing food inside your body to extract *energy* and *nutrients*.

Food groups

A healthy, balanced diet includes some food from each group shown below. You should mostly eat foods from the biggest section, and only have foods from the smallest section occasionally.

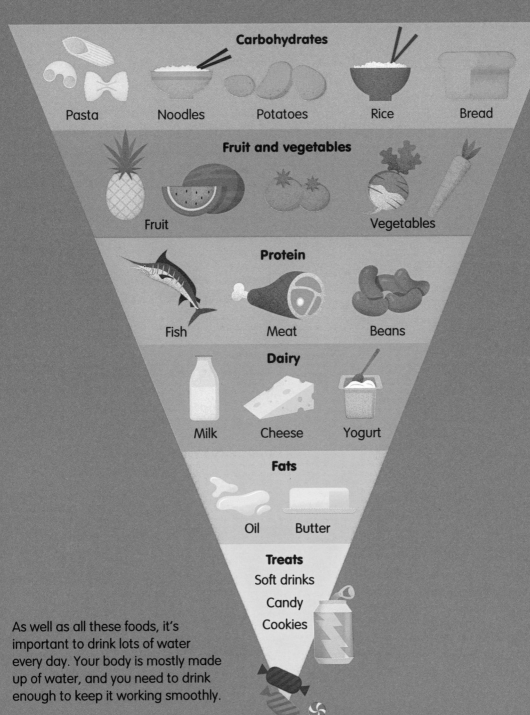

Carbohydrates

Pasta   Noodles   Potatoes   Rice   Bread

Fruit and vegetables

Fruit   Vegetables

Protein

Fish   Meat   Beans

Dairy

Milk   Cheese   Yogurt

Fats

Oil   Butter

Treats
Soft drinks
Candy
Cookies

As well as all these foods, it's important to drink lots of water every day. Your body is mostly made up of water, and you need to drink enough to keep it working smoothly.

digestive system The organs in your body, including the stomach and intestines, responsible for *digesting* food.

electrolytes Electrically-charged particles in your blood that your body needs to work properly. They are lost during exercise so need to be replenished afterwards.

energy Capacity to do work. Energy enables you to move, breathe, walk and talk.

enzymes Biological substances that speed up reactions, such as those involved in *digesting* food.

fats A food group of high-*energy* substances, found in foods such as oil, butter, cheese and meat.

fermentation A process that turns *sugar* into gas and alcohol.

fiber A part of foods, especially *grains* and *fruits*, that cannot be digested and contains no nutrients, but that helps the *digestive system* to work properly.

flavors When you eat, the *taste* and smell of the food are what make its distinct flavor.

flavorings Substances added to food to give different or stronger *flavors*. Can be natural, such as *herbs* and *spices*, or artificial.

food groups The loose categories foods can be divided into. You should eat some food from each group every day, to get *energy* and the right balance of *nutrients*.

fruit and vegetables A *food group* consisting of edible parts of plants. Fruits are the parts of plants that contain the seeds. The term 'vegetables' tends to apply to the leaves or roots.

gelatin A substance, usually made from parts of animals, that is used to give foods such as jelly and candies a firm consistency and make them set.

grafting Attaching parts of two trees together. In farming this is often used to create new varieties of a fruit.

grains A group of grass plants grown for food, including wheat, corn and rice. Also known as **cereals**.

harvesting Collecting ripe crops from fields or greenhouses.

herbs Aromatic *seasonings* from the leaves of some plants, for example basil or mint.

hormones *Chemical* messengers that take signals from one part of your body to another.

hydroponics A system of *agriculture* in which plants are grown in water rather than soil.

legumes A group of *vegetables* including beans and peas, which are rich in *protein*.

livestock Farmed animals used for meat, milk, and other products.

Maillard reaction A reaction that takes place whenever a food turns brown as it cooks. This adds to the *flavor* of cooked foods.

metabolism The *chemical* processes that use energy in food to create energy in your body.

Michelin Star A prestigious award given to restaurants for exceptional food and service.

nutrients A general term for the substances in food or drink that provide some benefit to your health.

nutrition Taking *nutrients* into your body.

preservation Preparing or keeping food and drinks in a way that prevents them from

spoiling. Common methods of preservation include refrigeration and canning.

protein A **food group** important for helping your body grow and repair muscles. It's found primarily in meat, fish and **legumes**.

recipes The lists of ingredients and instructions for preparing particular dishes.

salt Small white crystals of sodium chloride, used as a **seasoning**. Your body needs a small amount of salt to work properly, but too much is bad for you.

salty One of the five main **tastes**. The tongue's simplest receptors detect **salt** in food.

savory See **umami**.

scurvy An illness caused by a deficiency of vitamin C.

seasonings Substances such as **salt** and pepper added to food to enhance its **flavor**.

selective breeding The process where farmers choose the plants and animals with the best characteristics to breed together, to create even better new plants and animals.

sour One of the five main **tastes**. A sharp taste, found in foods such as lemons and vinegar.

spices Aromatic **seasonings** from any part of a plant (apart from the leaf), for example the bark or seed.

spoiling When food goes bad and is no longer edible.

staples Foods, usually **carbohydrates**, that provide the majority of **calories** people eat on a daily basis. They vary from region to region, but include rice, wheat, corn and potatoes.

sugar A **sweet** substance extracted from plants such as sugar cane or beet. Often added to foods to make them sweeter.

sweet One of the five main **tastes**, which indicates the presence of **sugar** and means that a food contains lots of **energy**.

tastes The basic sensations associated with food, detected by **tastebuds** on the tongue – **sweet**, **salty**, **umami**, **bitter** and **sour**.

tastebuds Tiny organs on your tongue and in your throat, which contain receptors that allow you to detect a food's **taste**.

toxic A substance that is poisonous and harmful to your body is toxic.

umami Also known as 'savory', one of the five main **tastes**. It's particularly found in cheeses and meats.

vegetables See **fruit and vegetables**.

vitamin deficiency Having too little of a vitamin in your body, leading to illness or weakness.

vitamins and minerals Substances found in certain foods that do different jobs in your body to keep it healthy. Eating a balanced diet ensures you get enough of all of them.

yeast A tiny, single-celled fungus that is added to breads to make them rise.

Index

Page numbers where you can find out most about a subject are shown in **bold**.

A

acids, 21, 31, 35, 62, 69, 79
ackee fruit, 78
addiction, 27
adenosines, 108
advertising, 106-107
afternoon tea, 56
alcohol, 25
allicin, 52
ambergris, 102
amino acids, 86
androstenone, 84, 85
anthocyanins, 26
antibodies, 5
antioxidants, 109
appetite, 16
apples, 42, 59, 68, 113
apricots, 59
arachibutyrophobia, 69
aroma compounds, 86, 87
arsenic, 29
ascorbic acid, 35
asparagus, 12, 28, 112
astronauts, 17
autolysis, 103
avocados, 4, 59, 70, 96

B

babies, **4-5**, 12, 75
bacon, 17, 38, 71, 86-87
bacteria, 39, 46, 52, 53, 62, 63, 69, 90, 99, **103**, 105, 120
bananas, 51, 59, 70, 74, **82**
beans, 13, 29, 39, 70, 90, 96

bees, 14, **113**
beta-carotene, 26, 75
beta-glucans, 91
biscuits, sea, 50
blood, 4, 15, 18, 19, 28, 48, 68, 75, 89
blood, pressure, 31
blood sugar, 16, 18, 19
boiling, 38
bones, 13, 28, 91
bowel, 21
brain, 9, 12, 21, 27, 45, 108, 116
bread, 4, 18, 19, **24-25**, 38, 83, 97, 103
breadfruit, 109
breast milk, 4-5
brigade system, 54-55
brine, 62
British Royal Navy, 34, 35
broccoli, 13, 59, 84
bromelain, 31
burgers, 37, 65, 97
burritos, 96-97
butter, 38, 70, 93, 103
   yak, 67

C

cacao beans, 72, 73, 97, 110
caffeine, 108
cake, 56, 57, **70**
calcium, 13, 28, 99
calories, 6, **30**, 109, 120
camels, 11
canning, 63
capsaicin, 52, 76

carbohydrates, 4, 18, 39, 46, 83, 109, 120, 121
   complex, 18, 39
carbon dioxide, 25
carotenosis, 75
carrots, 12, **32-33**, 74, 75, 98
carvone, 100
cassava root, 79
castoreum, 102
cauliflower, 95
cells, 12, 19, 21, 26, 28, 37
champagne, 92-93
cheese, 4, 28, 45, 53, 93, 95, 97, 107
chefs, 23, 47, **54-55**, 77, 78, 81, 95, 97, 111, 120
chemicals, 8, 14, 26, 28-29, 31, 33, 51, 61, 84, 86, 94, 95, 104, 108
chewing, 8, 21
chewing gum, **21**, 61, 102
chili, 52, **76**, 96
Chinese cuisine, 111
chlorine, 31
chlorophyll, 58, 108
chocolate, 14, 29, **72-73**, 95, 97
cholesterol, 16, 91, 120
cilantro, 7, 84, 97
clay, 99
cobalt, 28
cochineal, 102
cocoa nibs, 73
coffee, 50, 66, **108**
collagen, 29
Columbus, Christopher, 96
companion planting, 90

constipation, 17, 99
cookbooks, 7
cookies, 30, 27, 68
copper, 29, 99
corn, 6, 15, 22, 90, 91
cornflakes, 15
cows, 11, 36, 37, 116-117
cream, 56-57, 95, 98
  sour, 7, 97
crops, 6, 11, 22, 24, 33, 90,
  120
cucumbers, 62, 68, 95
cumin, 7
curing, 62

D

dairy, 120, 121 *see also*
cheese, yogurt, milk
desserts, 45, 55, 102, 115
diet, 6, 20, 34, 46, 91,
  118, 119
  low residue, 17
digestion, 16, 18, 21, 69,
  120, 121
digestive system, **16**, 21, 39,
  68, 122
dill, 100
diseases, 12, 26, 29, 34-35,
  42, 82, 91, 101 *see also*
  infections
  rickets, 13
  scurvy, 34-35, 123
DNA, 12, 33, 84
dopamine, 27
dough, 25, 40
droughts, 11
durian fruit, 51

E

eel, 95
eggs, 4, 13, 17, 23, 29, 38, 55,
  57, 68, 70, 71, 103, 115
electrolytes, 88-89
elements, **28-29**, 74
energy, 4, 5, 13, 18-19, **30**,
  36, 44, 88, 89, 109, 122
enzymes, **14**, 31, 39, 69, 75,
  103, 122
Escoffier, Georges-Auguste,
  54
ethylene, 58, 59
explosives, 30, 31
eyesight, 12, 26

F

farming, 22, 32-33, 37, 42,
  58, 65, 90, 91, 92, 93, 94,
  104-105, 113
fat, 4, 7, 17, 65, 70, 77, 87,
  103, 121, 122
fermentation, 66, 72, 77,
  79, 122
fiber, **16**, 17, 19, 91, 122
fish, 13, 36, 54, 62, 71, 77, 78
  sword, 29
fishing, 10
flavor, **8-9**, 61, 95, 122
flavoring, 61, 102, 122
flavorists, 61
Fleming, Alexander, 53
flour, 24, 50, 70, **83**, 98
fluids, neo-Newtonian, 48
  Newtonian, 48
  non-Newtonian, 48
folate, 26 *see also* vitamin B_9
folic acid *see* vitamin B_9

food dye, 102
food pairing, 95
food security, 109
food stylists, 106
fortified food, 15
frankenburger, 37
freezing, 62
fries, 10, 97, 107
fructose, 14
fruit, 4, 26, 43, 44, 59, 75, 103,
  113, 121, 122
  citrus, 12, 34-35, 102
  see also lemons, limes,
  oranges
fruit juice, 68
fugu (pufferfish) 78
fungi, 25, 52, 84, 85, 91

G

gallium, 29
garlic, 7, 52, 65, 111
gelatin, **75**, 102, 122
genes, 33, 82
genetic modification, (GM)
  32-33
ginger, 52, 111
gingerol, 52
Giugiaro, Giorgetto, 41
gluconic acid, 69
glucose, 14
grafting, 42, 122
grains, 16, 25, 46, 122
grapes, 43, 92

H

heart, 26, 76, 91
herbs, 100, 122
honey, 14, 52, **69**, 70, 93

hormones, 37, **116**, 122
huitlacoche, 91
hydrogen peroxide, 69
hydrogen sulfide, 39
hydroponics, 104-105, 122

I

ice cream, 61, 101, 102, 106
immune system, 29
infections, 5, 53, 91 *see also*
  diseases
insects, 50, 64, **65**, 94, 102
insulin, 18, 19
intestines, 13, 16, 39, 52
invertase, 14
iron, 15, 28, 99, 109
isoamyl acetate, 51

J

jam, 56-57, 98
Japanese cuisine, 77
jelly beans, 18
juniper, 7

K

katsuobushi, 77
keratin, 29
ketchup, 48-49
kidneys, 13
kilojoules, 30
kiwi fruit, 59, 75, 95
knives, 111

L

lanolin, 102
leeks, 7

lemons, 20, 34-35
lentils, 93
limes, 34, 35, 97
Lind, Dr. James, 34
liquorice, 7, 95
liver, 19
livestock, 11, 122
lutein, 26
lycopene, 26
lysine, 91

M

mackerel, 110
magnesium, 99, 109
magnets, 15
mangos, 95
margarine, 98
Mayans, 110
meat, 4, 17, 28, 36, 37, 46,
  47, 54, 62, 65, 71, 103,
  106, 111
  beef, 29, 36, 65, 97
  chicken, 13, 28, 36, 68,
  79, 97
  lamb, 7, 93
  pork, 17, 97
  turkey, 36
melatonin, 116, 117
melons, 43
memory, 26, 27
menthol, 52
mercury, 29
meringues, 115
Michelin Stars, **80-81**, 122
milk, **4-5**, 11, 57, 62, 67, 68,
  73, 76, 97, 103, 116-117
  breast, 4
  camels, 11
  cows, 11
  formula, 4

minerals, 4, 15, **28-29**, 65,
  88, 99, 109, 123
mint, 52, 67, **100**
miracle berry, 20
miraculin, 20
molybdenum, 28
Monsieur Mangetout, 114
mold, 53, 72, 77, 103
mouth, 8
muscles, 4, 29, 31, **36**, 37,
  88, 89
mushrooms, 29, 84, 91
myoglobin, 36

N

NASA, 17, 104
Native Americans, 90, 97
nectar, 14, 113
nickel, 29
nitrates, 87, 90
nitrogen, 29, 104
nose, 8
nutrients, 4, 5, 16, 26, 91, 99,
  103, 104, 122
nuts, 4, 12, 16, 46, 70
  brazil, 28, 74
  cashew, 79

O

oats, 29, 70
oligosaccharides, 39
olive oil, 52, 97
olives, 88, 89
onions, 21
oranges, **58**, 68
oryza sativa, 6
oxygen, 15, 28, 83, 103
oysters, 29, 95

P

packaging, 63
pancreas, 18
papayas, 75
parasites, 99
parsley, 28
passion fruit, 95
pasta, 4, 19, **40-41**, 97
Pasteur, Louis, 62
pasteurization, 62
peanut butter, 48, 68,
   69, 103
peas, 28, 95
penicillin, 53
peppers, 12, 76, 96 *see
   also* chili
Periodic Table, 28-29
pesticides, 37, 99
phosphorus, 104
pica, 114
pickling, 62
picocuries, 74
pineapples, 31, 75
plants, 6, 22, 32, 33, 42, 58,
   60, 61, 66, 72, 74, 82, 90,
   91, 94, 97, 104, 105, 109, 113
plaque, 46
poisons, 29, 78-79, 99, 108
pollen, 113
poop, 16
potassium, 74, 104, 109
potatoes, 68, 70, 71, 74, 97,
   98, 108
pregnancy, 12, 99
preservation, 62-63, 122
protein, 4, 17, 31, 36, 37, 38,
   65, 75, 86, 109, 121, 123
psychologists, 44, 45

R

radioactivity, 74
radium, 28, 74
rancidification, 103
reactions
   irreversible, 38
   Maillard, 38, 86, 122
   reversible, 38
receptors
   smell, 8, 9
   taste, 8, 9, 20, 84
recipes, 7, 24, 61, 65, 89, 98,
   102, 115, 123
refrigerators, 43
restaurants, 44, 54-55, 80-81
reward pathway, 27
rhubarb, 79
riboflavin, *see* vitamin B_2
rice, 4, **6**, 29, 67, 77, 97
rubidium, 28

S

saffron, 60
sailors, 34-35, 50
saliva, 69, 101
salmon, 95
salt, 7, **31**, 62, 67, 110, 123
sandwiches, 56
sashimi, 78
scones, 56-57
Scoville Scale, 76
Second World War, 98
seeds, 4, 12, 22, 24, 32, 33,
   46, 78, 79, 98, 104, 107, 109
selective breeding, **32-33**,
   123
semolina, 7

senses, 8-9
serotonin, 116, 117
shallots, 7
sharks, 10
shelf life, 103
shellac, 102
silicon, 29
skeleton, 13
skin, 26, 29, 31
sleep, 108, 116-117
smell, 8-9, 86, 87
sodas, 61, 68, 106
sodium chloride *see* salt
sodium, 31
soil, 99, **104-105**
solanine, 108
soup, 10, 40, 55
space, 17, 104-105
spices, 60, 67, 111
spinach, 12
spoiling, 103, 123
sports drinks, 88-89
sprouts, brussel, 13, 84
squash, 12, 90
staple foods, 6, 123
steak, 17, 28, 106
stomach, 16, 39, 52
strawberries, 12, 45, 56, 57, 61,
   95, 106
strontium, 28
sucrose, 14
sugar, 14, 18-19, 20, 25, 39, 44,
   46, 48, 67, 70, 73, 83, 86, 89,
   98, 115, 123
   cane, 6
   crash, 19
   fructose, 14
   glucose, 14
   simple, 18
   sucrose, 14

sulfur, 21, 29
sulfuric acid, 21
sweetener, 20
sweets, 18, 61, 102
Szent-Györgyi, Albert, 35

T

tapioca, 67, 79
tastebuds, 8, 20, 123
taste, sense of, 8-9
tastes, basic, 8-9, 123
  bitter, 9, 120
  salty, 9, 89, 123
  sour, 9, 20, 123
  sweet, 9, 20, 89, 123
  umami, 8, 77, 123
tea, 56, **66-67**, 94, 95, 110
  brewing, 67
tears, 21
teeth, 28, **46**
terpenes, 94
terroir, 92
thiamine, *see* vitamin B₁
Titanic, 112

toast, 38, 64
tofu, 4, 70
tomatoes, 48, 59, 96, 97,
  104, 105
tongue, 8, 31
toques, 23
tortillas, 96
toxins *see* poisons
truffles, 84, 85
tryptophan, 116-117

V

vacuum packing, 63
vanadium, 28
vanilla, 102
vegetables, 4, 16, 26, 90, 103, 121,
122
vinegar, 20
vitamins, 4, **12-13**, 123
  A, 12
  B₁, 13
  B₂, 13
  B₉, 12
  B₁₂, 28

  C, 12, 26, 35, 109
  D, 13
  E, 12
  K, 13
  deficiency, 13, 123

W

water, 4, 6, 7, 11, 16, 21, 24, 31,
  40, 48, 50, **68**, 104, 105, 121
watermelons, 43
wheat, 22, 24, 28, 40
whisking, 115
wholegrain foods, 19
wine, 62, 92-93

Y

yams, 110
yeast, **25**, 103, 123
yogurt, 45, 70

Z

zinc, 29

Internet links

For links to websites where you can discover more
surprising food facts with video clips, quizzes and activities,
go to the Usborne Quicklinks website at
www.usborne.com/quicklinks and enter
the keywords: **100 food things**.

Here are some of the things you can do at the
websites we recommend:

• Discover why your stomach rumbles
• Find out about bark that people love to add to oatmeal
• See where your food comes from and how many
countries you rely on for your daily meals
• Fight bacteria that lives on food and can make you sick

Please follow the internet safety guidelines at the Usborne
Quicklinks website. We recommend that children are
supervised while on the internet.

It takes a brigade...
to make a book.

Research and writing
Sam Baer, Rachel Firth, Rose Hall,
Alice James, Jerome Martin

Design
Jamie Ball, Freya Harrison, Amy Manning,
Lenka Hrehova, Alice Reese, Vickie Robinson

Illustration
Federico Mariani
Parko Polo

Expert fact-checking
Claudia Havranek
Jenny Chandler

U.S. editor: Carrie Armstrong   Series editor: Ruth Brocklehurst   Series designer: Stephen Moncrieff

First published in 2017 by Usborne Publishing Ltd., Usborne House, 83–85 Saffron Hill, London,
EC1N 8RT, United Kingdom. www.usborne.com Copyright © 2017 Usborne Publishing Ltd. The name
Usborne and the devices ♀ ⊕ are Trade Marks of Usborne Publishing Ltd. All rights reserved. No part of this
publication may be reproduced, stored in any retrieval system, or transmitted in any form or by any means,
electronic, mechanical, photocopying, recording or otherwise, without the prior permission
of the publisher. Printed in UAE. AE. First published in America in 2017.